Also by Leigh Russell

Poppy Mystery Tales
Barking Up the Right Tree
Barking Mad
Poppy Takes the Lead

Geraldine Steel Mysteries
Cut Short
Road Closed
Dead End
Death Bed
Stop Dead
Fatal Act
Killer Plan
Murder Ring
Deadly Alibi
Class Murder
Death Rope
Rogue Killer
Deathly Affair
Deadly Revenge
Evil Impulse
Deep Cover
Guilt Edged
Fake Alibi
Final Term
Without Trace
Revenge Killing
Deadly Will

Ian Peterson Murder Investigations
Cold Sacrifice
Race to Death
Blood Axe

Lucy Hall Mysteries
Journey to Death
Girl in Danger
The Wrong Suspect

The Adulterer's Wife
Suspicion

POPPY's *Christmas* CRACKER

LEIGH RUSSELL

A POPPY MYSTERY TALE

cmc

First published in 2024 by
The Crime & Mystery Club,
an imprint of Oldcastle Books Ltd.,
Harpenden, UK

crimeandmysteryclub.co.uk
@CrimeMystClub

ISBN
978-0-85730-600-5 (Paperback)
978-0-85730-601-2 (eBook)

2 4 6 8 10 9 7 5 3 1

Typeset in 12 on 14.85pt Monotype Sabon
by Avocet Typeset, Bideford, Devon, EX39 2BP
Printed and bound in Great Britain by Clays Ltd, Elcograf S.p.A.

This story is for Poppy

It is also dedicated to Michael, Jo, Phillipa, Phil, Rian, Kezia and Poppy's cousin, Lily

1

IT WAS LUCKY FOR me that my boss was also my best friend. Anyone looking through the window of the Sunshine Tea Shoppe at the beginning of November might have seen the two of us having fun festooning the windows of the café with tinsel and other seasonal decorations. Hannah hoped the two months leading up to Christmas would be busy for the tea rooms. Although we were rarely short of customers, she often worried that her business was close to financial ruin. The problem, as I saw it, was partly due to her own good nature, because she often waived the bill for customers she thought were struggling financially. I had given up trying to convince her that her open-handed approach was threatening to turn the café into a magnet for the needy.

'Isn't that the point?' she had said the last time we had discussed the situation. 'Needy means they need help, and that's what we're giving them.'

'You're always complaining about paying the bills,' I pointed out. I didn't add that my wages hadn't increased in the three years I had been working for her.

'The one has nothing to do with the other,' she replied. 'Giving away a few quid here and there isn't going to affect the rates or my other horrendous bills.'

I wasn't sure her argument made sense, but merely shrugged, muttering that she was the boss and it was her business on the line.

As we strung up the decorations, Poppy jumped around at our heels, barking with excitement. Eager to join in our new game, my little Jack Tzu darted off several times with a colourful string of bunting trailing behind her while my friend chased after her, ignoring my protestations that there was really no point; Poppy was too fast to catch. Time and again, she dodged Hannah's outstretched hands. A cross between a Jack Russell Terrier and a Shih Tzu, Poppy was mischievous but undeniably cute, with white legs and tail, and light brown patches on her back. Her bright-black eyes and affectionate nature made her utterly adorable. Even people who were not usually dog lovers warmed to her. Not only faster on her feet than a human being, she was also more intelligent than many people I met.

Three years had passed since I inherited Poppy from my great aunt, along with my picturesque cottage. I had been enchanted by Rosecroft from the moment I saw its soft yellow-stone walls with honeysuckle and clematis growing around the door and a low white-picket fence marking the border of the garden. No doubt my great aunt had done her best, but she had been frail by the time she died and must have struggled to maintain the property. It was old and packed with little cupboards and crannies which were difficult to keep free of dust that appeared to burgeon from nowhere, accumulating in corners and on shelves that were difficult to reach. After years of neglect, the interior of my new home had taken me weeks to clean, but enjoying the good fortune to own a home of my own had made it worth all the effort. And even though Poppy had been foisted on me without my consent, we had quickly become devoted to one another, until it was impossible to imagine my life without her.

Once we had finished decorating for Christmas, the tea rooms looked like a magical cave, a spectacular riot of sparkling colours, the yellow walls hung with strands of glittering crimson and gold tinsel, adorned with bright shiny red and green baubles. The merry colours of Christmas seemed to reflect Hannah's cheerful nature. She ran her tea shop with unflagging good humour, extending her warm hospitality to everyone, and welcoming strangers as though they were old friends, in a happy combination of sound business acumen and natural affability. Her tea shop itself was the result of a similar happy combination of circumstance and aspiration, her divorce from a wealthy ex-husband having given her enough money to fulfil her dream of opening a café. Tall and statuesque, her natural blonde curls seemed in keeping with the yellow tea shop, as though it was natural for her to be working there. My unruly red hair didn't match the décor as well, and my mother was certainly convinced I was out of place there. She thought I should be striving to better myself and disapproved of my working as a waitress, but I considered myself lucky to be working in such a friendly tea shop, in a picturesque village. With Poppy as my constant and loyal companion, my life was very nearly perfect. All that was missing was a boyfriend.

Reactions to our decorations varied. Hannah's boyfriend, Adam, barely acknowledged our efforts, merely grunting when Hannah asked his opinion, but many of our customers complimented us on our efforts. The women, especially, gazed around, smiling and remarking how lovely it looked. I repeated all the accolades to Hannah, and we were both gratified by the appreciation. On the first Sunday of November, we served the last of the teatime orders for the day and closed with barely enough time to clear up before the lights along the High Street were due to be switched on. We stepped outside and joined a crowd of local residents who were standing around, stamping their feet and chattering noisily, little clouds of condensed breath faintly visible in front of their faces. Hannah had confided to me that she was a little disappointed by Adam's ready dismissal of our tinsel and fairy lights. Predictably, he had declined to come along to witness the annual turning on of the Christmas lights.

Although I was keen to watch the lights come on, it was growing increasingly chilly, and before long my fingers and toes began to hurt. Hannah was as eager to leave as I was; she wanted to go home to Adam. Still, it seemed churlish to complain about the weather. It was November, and not especially cold for the time of year. Nevertheless, I waited impatiently as the road and both pavements filled up with spectators gathering near the enormous Christmas tree. Other than suffering from the cold, my other concern was that Poppy might be scared by so many onlookers crammed together in the centre of the village. She liked people, as a rule, but the villagers were out in force today, all packed into a small stretch of the High Street. So far she seemed happy enough, settled between my feet. As we were waiting, Hannah murmured that it was a good thing we had put the finishing touches to our decorations in the tea shop the previous evening, as everyone could see into the Sunshine Tea Shoppe from the street. I agreed the place looked stunning, and she beamed.

The Christmas tree in the High Street was paid for by the local retailers, with a contribution from the council. None of us knew how much money had been donated by the council. According to rumour, it wasn't much. Nevertheless, we all cheered when the mayor stepped forward to turn on the lights. As soon as the cheering and clapping started, I picked Poppy up and held her in my arms where she would feel safe. To be fair, the noisy applause was more for the lights than the official who had deigned to come along and flick a switch, but he smiled and waved his hand graciously before making a speech which was thankfully short. It was almost impossible to hear his voice above the excited chatter on the crowded pavements, but as no one wanted to hear what he was saying, it didn't matter. All the retailers had made an effort to coordinate their decorations, and when the lights were turned on, the whole street glowed and glimmered with strings of red and green lights.

Even the empty store across the road from our tea shop sported coloured lights strung across its frontage, thanks to the shopkeepers on either side. Until the summer it had been a gift shop, aimed mainly at tourists passing through the village, but everyone knew the owners had been struggling for a while. Close to retirement age, once their lease ran out they had been pleased to close down. The premises had only been empty for a few months when the estate agent's 'To Let' sign was taken down. We were all curious to know who was taking it over, but even Maud who ran the village grocery store, and was usually up to date with local gossip, couldn't tell us. The uncertainty gave rise to several rumours, which became increasingly outlandish as time passed. For no apparent reason, one of our customers was convinced it would be a shop selling kitchenware. The owner of the village hair and beauty salon was worried that a second hair salon was opening in the vacant premises. We were assured by a number of people that it was going to be a tattoo parlour. Hannah and I suspected that particular rumour had come from a single deluded person who had speculated about it to a number of their neighbours, each of whom had mentioned it to several other villagers. Someone else assured us a shop selling risqué lingerie would be opening its doors opposite us very soon. In the meantime, we just had to wait and see.

The Christmas tree in the street looked beautiful, swathed in strings of golden lights interspersed with shining stars. There was a communal sigh as we saw it light up, glowing against the dark sky. People were laughing, jumping up and down in the cold, and rubbing their hands to warm them, while children careered along the central stretch of the road which had been closed to traffic. Every year the middle section of the High Street was cordoned off for the Christmas tree and the local children took that as an invitation to run wild on the open road. The closure was always controversial, as some retailers felt it affected their business when customers couldn't park right outside their shops. The counter argument to that was that when the streets were busy, drivers were unlikely to find a parking space on the High Street anyway, so it actually made no difference at all. Hannah didn't mind either way, but I preferred looking out at the Christmas tree than at cars driving past or parked on the street, and in any case the tree blocking the road probably attracted people who might pop into the tea shop for a hot drink and a cake.

While the mayor had been delivering his speech to the assembled villagers, Poppy had nestled quietly in my arms with her head against my shoulder. Her tail wagged cautiously, as though she could sense the excitement but wasn't quite sure what was going on. I suspected she was even less interested in all the Christmas lights and tinsel than Adam. When the mayor had finished, I had slipped the loop of Poppy's lead around my wrist, so I could put her down and join in the polite applause as he stepped down from his makeshift podium. Poppy settled down between my feet, watching the crowd, alert to every movement near us.

Above the confused hubbub of voices, the local pub landlord's stentorian cheering rang out like a foghorn through the mist. It was easy to spot the local policeman, Barry, who stood a head taller than most of the other villagers. His windswept straw-coloured hair appeared to have golden highlights in the glow from the Christmas lights. Remembering how keen Barry had been to go out with me, I smiled at him, but he didn't see me. Beside him, and just within my line of vision, Maud and Norman were standing hand in hand like young lovers, although neither of them would see sixty again. Norman, the village butcher, and Maud were due to be married soon. Hannah had been tasked with making a wedding cake for the occasion, which she had insisted neither Maud nor Norman was allowed to see. Maud had begged for just a peek at it, but Hannah was determined to keep it a secret. She had placed me under strict instructions not to betray even the smallest detail about the design. It was a rich fruitcake, which Hannah said would keep fresh, giving her time to work on it. She had spent hours making a stupendous creation, a tower comprising four cakes which diminished in size as the layers rose. Each was generously covered in white icing decorated with hundreds of delicately coloured sugar flowers all made by hand.

'Is there no end to your talents?' I asked Hannah, awestruck by her artistry.

Looking towards the tree, I caught sight of my friend, Toby. He had brought his mother, Naomi, to watch the lights being turned on, and the people standing in front of them had parted so she could watch the proceedings from her wheelchair. Almost hidden under a heap of blankets, she was grinning with excitement and nodding her head at something Toby was saying. Once a PE teacher, Naomi was no longer able to walk, thanks to a crippling condition, and she didn't get out much. She bore her physical affliction with cheerful fortitude, but it couldn't have been easy for her. Her life must have been quite tedious, most of the time. Attending an event like this must have made a welcome change for her, and she looked as excited as the children.

The only person I was dismayed to see in the crowd was Dana Flack, a reporter from the local paper who was always poking her nose into village business, scavenging for scraps of scandal to misrepresent in her gossipy reports. With crimson lipstick and a black beret, her tall figure and hunched posture were easy to spot in the crowd. Her piercing eyes roamed restlessly over the heads of the crowd, swooping down now and again to focus ferociously on an individual who had attracted her interest. Although I had no reason to hide from her, I shifted sideways to stand behind a tall man to shield myself from Dana's predatory stare.

With the Christmas lights on, the crowd began to disperse and the mayor departed to fulfil his next civic duty. He probably had more lights to switch on before he was finished for the day. He must have had a tiring schedule, coming up to Christmas, but he had the grace to look as though he was enjoying himself. Lifting Poppy up again, I made my way slowly through the thinning crowd. Leaving the High Street behind us, we headed for home. Poppy wriggled to be put down and trotted happily in front of me, stopping now and then to sniff the ground. She was particularly interested in clumps of weeds growing at the edge of the pavement, and favoured specific places to pause and pee. She was very particular about where she wanted to mark her territory or leave messages for other dogs. The rain had held off while the lights were switched on, but a light drizzle began to fall as we reached the lane where we lived, and we were both pleased to reach the shelter of home.

2

A WEEK OR SO after the lights were turned on in the High Street, the wedding of Maud and Norman looked set to go off without a hitch. There was a festive atmosphere of barely suppressed excitement in the packed church as we waited for the ceremony to begin. Everyone had dressed up for the occasion, and I was glad I had listened to Hannah and worn a long skirt with a coordinating sparkly top. Hannah looked stunning in a close-fitting black dress. She and Adam were a good-looking couple. Even Barry looked unusually smart in a jacket that hugged his broad shoulders. As for Maud, she was resplendent in a long frilly raspberry-coloured frock, her naturally grey hair transformed into rigid blonde curls. We all agreed in her presence that she was a beautiful bride. Opinions varied when she was no longer in earshot, with some people wondering why she wanted her natural hair to resemble a wig, and others questioning her gaudy choice of wedding outfit.

Despite these few critical comments behind her back, we were all very complimentary to her face. The residents of Ashton Mead prided themselves on being a supportive community, and everyone wanted to be kind to Maud on her special day. Perhaps with Christmas approaching, the guests were particularly keen to share the spirit of goodwill. Everyone, that is, except the groom's former partner. During the ceremony, when the vicar asked if anyone knew of a reason why Maud and Norman should not be joined in holy matrimony, a woman leapt to her feet, shrieking a shrill accusation.

'Norman can't marry that old bat,' she cried out. 'He promised to marry me soon as his divorce came through. You get away from her this minute, Norman Norris. She must be seventy if she's a day. He oughta be making an honest woman of me, not running off with some old hag all tarted up in pink!'

'Didn't I tell you me and Patsy were never married!' Norman cried out triumphantly to the congregation at large, before swinging his considerable bulk round to address the intruder. 'Sling your hook, Patsy, I'm with Maud now.' With that, he turned back to his bride and leaned down to give her a resounding kiss on the lips.

'We haven't reached that part yet,' the vicar stammered, clearly put off his stride by the noisy interruption to the proceedings.

'Sorry about that, vicar,' Norman said, duly chastened. 'I don't know what Patsy's doing here. She wasn't invited.'

There was a brief scuffle at the back of the church as Norman's aggrieved former partner was escorted out, screeching about mutton dressed as lamb. Adam pointed out that was an appropriate comment to make about the bride of the village butcher, causing ripples of laughter as his remark was repeated around the guests. With the gatecrasher removed, the congregation stopped laughing and settled down, and the vicar resumed. Maud seemed completely unfazed by the disturbance and remained resolutely radiant. Even the vicar's sermon failed to dim her smile as he rambled on about fruitful unions, which hardly seemed appropriate, given the age of the couple. Still, all in all, it was a jolly affair, and certainly entertaining. At last the address came to an end, the ceremony was over, and Hannah and Cliff, the landlord of The Plough, hurried to the pub to remove covers from platters of food and open bottles of bubbly. Leaving me in charge of the Sunshine Tea Shoppe, Hannah had spent the week baking bread and buns, sausage rolls and quiches, doughnuts and scones and cupcakes. The trestle tables in the bar area were packed with enough food to satisfy the inhabitants of several villages.

While the wedding buffet was being prepared, and the local photographer was busy taking pictures of the happy couple and their friends and family, I slipped away to fetch Poppy. Entering the pub, she stood transfixed, sniffing the diverse food smells, while Hannah bustled about, straightening the display around the centrepiece, the wedding cake which towered above the sausage rolls and finger sandwiches like a colossus. With everyone around us drinking and tucking into the buffet, I shared a cocktail sausage with Poppy who devoured her morsels ravenously. The salt in the tasty treat was no good for her, but it was hard to resist her pleading eyes. As it happened, she had eaten a good breakfast that morning before I left for the wedding ceremony but, like everyone else, she was entitled to enjoy the party.

'I hope I've made enough,' Hannah said, stepping back to survey her handiwork critically.

'Don't be daft,' I laughed. 'There's enough food here to feed an army.'

We had no time to say anything else before Adam swept her away to meet a friend of his, and I took another sausage to share with Poppy. The beaming landlord, Cliff, and his barmaid, Michelle, were kept busy pulling pints and pouring glasses of wine. Michelle's boyfriend, Toby, went behind the bar to lend a hand. He said something to Michelle and she laughed, tossing her hair back from her thin face and smiling at him. Seeing him plant a kiss on her cheek, I felt a slight flicker of regret. When I had first arrived in the village, Toby and I had engaged in a casual flirtation. At one point I had even hoped we might become an item. But months passed, and our relationship had never developed beyond a warm friendship. Then Michelle had arrived and put an end to my speculation. My initial disappointment had quickly faded, especially as I liked Michelle. Placid and quiet, she was very different to me, and seeing how happy Toby was with her, I realised he and I would never have been compatible as a couple.

While Toby chatted with Michelle, I circulated, talking to people I knew, and watching Hannah enjoy the occasion as people complimented her on the buffet.

'I'm stuffed,' Adam said, pulling a chair over and joining me, closely followed by Hannah. He grinned at her. 'You've done us proud,' he told her and she smiled.

'Emily helped,' she murmured.

'Only by serving tea and cakes in the tea shop,' I protested. 'You did all this.' I waved my hand around to indicate the buffet, narrowly missing knocking Norman's arm and upsetting his beer all over Maud's frock. She didn't notice, and Norman winked at me and put his finger on his lips.

Once the eating and drinking frenzy slowed down, Maud and Norman went and stood in front of the bar to the accompaniment of cheers, after which there were toasts and applause and speeches and more cheers, which grew increasingly rowdy, and everyone had a thoroughly enjoyable time. Finally, the moment came to cut the cake. Norman picked up a long-bladed knife with the easy familiarity of one accustomed to chopping meat. Maud placed her hand on top of his just as he made a sudden swift slicing movement with the knife. By now very tipsy, and already teetering on high heels, Maud lost her balance and fell forward onto the cake. With a faint popping of cracking icing and a wheezing sound, the wedding cake crumbled beneath her, scattering flecks of icing and shattered sugar flowers over the remains of the buffet. With a yelp of delight, Poppy darted forward to hoover up crumbs from the floor. I grabbed her and lifted her out of harm's way, as the cake was packed with dried fruits including raisins which are potentially toxic for dogs. To placate her, I gave her a whole sausage, dusted with flecks of icing, which she gobbled down ecstatically. Norman helped restore his giggling bride to a reasonably upright position, and she hung on his burly arm, smiling adoringly up at him. The cake, unfortunately, was a write off.

'It's lucky the photographer took pictures of it before it was ruined,' I murmured to Hannah.

I didn't add that the destruction of the wedding cake was probably a blessing in disguise; at least the guests had an excuse not to eat rich sugary cake on top of everything else. I, for one, wasn't sure my stomach could have handled it. At last, the guests had almost all left, apart from a few dedicated drinkers who lingered in the pub until closing time. Cliff and Michelle began gathering up the glasses while Hannah and I packed away any food we could salvage for the café. Toby and Adam were supposed to be helping us, but they only got in our way and were finally persuaded to sit down together over a last pint while Hannah and I got on with the task of clearing up.

Cliff declared himself satisfied with his takings for the day, and before we left, he booked Hannah to cater the Christmas party at the pub. When I first arrived in the village, the pub had offered hot food in the bar every day. Since his previous barmaid had been arrested, which was a whole other story, Cliff had withdrawn the menu in the bar area, and now only sold packets of crisps and nuts there. Customers who wanted to sit down for a proper meal could do so in the small restaurant area of the pub between seven and nine in the evening. With the success of the wedding party, and Cliff asking Hannah to supply a cold buffet for the Christmas party, she was pleased to have the work, even at short notice, and so it was agreed on the spot. Most of the village would be celebrating at home on Christmas Day, but at least those who lived alone could enjoy a communal party at the pub on Christmas Eve. The philanthropic aspect of the idea appealed to Hannah, while Cliff was no doubt calculating the profit he stood to make behind the bar.

Having made the arrangement with Hannah, Cliff returned to his clearing up, leaving me and my friends to discuss the Christmas Eve party. As well as that, the children who lived in the village were all invited to a children's party at the pub at the beginning of December, and we would need a Father Christmas to hand out gifts.

'Who would like to volunteer to be Father Christmas this year?' Hannah asked, looking around at Adam, Toby and Barry.

Adam shook his head vigorously. Toby mumbled that he would probably be busy, helping out behind the bar. Barry fidgeted and looked at the floor. Adam suggested that Cliff, with his portly figure and loud voice, was an obvious choice, but the pub landlord said that, although he would like to oblige, he would be needed behind the bar. It didn't really matter who played the part, as he – or she – would be concealed behind a red outfit. Adam added that under a red jacket even a slim woman could be padded out to create an illusion of a large jolly man. He looked directly at me as he spoke, but I quickly scotched that idea, pointing out that a female voice would destroy any illusion. A heated discussion followed, with many protestations and downright refusals from Adam and Toby and every other man in the bar. In the end, in his absence, Norman the butcher was volunteered for the role. As a tall stout man with a booming voice, he was certainly an ideal candidate for the role. He would be informed of our decision on his return from his honeymoon, when hopefully he would be in too cheerful a frame of mind to refuse our suggestion.

'He's going to love doing it,' Adam said confidently, and Toby and Barry nodded.

Now they were no longer under pressure to volunteer, they all agreed it would be a fun role to play.

'Who knows?' Hannah said. 'Norman might even be pleased that we thought of him. Now, does anyone know where we can find the costume from last year, or do we need to order a new one? We don't have much time.'

'Do we even know what size he is?' Michelle called out from behind the bar.

'That's a good point,' Toby replied. 'We can't have Santa bursting out of his red outfit.'

'Just get the biggest one we can find,' I replied. 'It doesn't matter if it's too big.'

'It can hardly be too big,' Adam said.

Since no one had actually asked Norman, we discussed whether he might refuse to take on the role and decided that Maud would be the best person to persuade him to agree. With an awkward shrug, Barry agreed to speak to Maud to help make sure Norman went along with our plans. Barry was her nephew, but since he had been orphaned at a young age, Maud had brought him up as if he was her own son and she was as devoted to him as any mother could have been. We were all sure that he would be able to prevail on her to support our idea.

'She may have plans of her own over Christmas,' Barry murmured, but no one paid any attention to his reservations.

'If anyone can persuade her, you can,' Hannah said with an air of finality.

'You have to,' I pleaded with him. 'It's really important.'

'Do it for the children,' Hannah added.

Barry glanced anxiously at me and nodded, as we all knew he would. His crush on me was no secret, and a word from me was often enough to sway his opinion, at least in trivial matters. Not that our choice for Father Christmas could be considered trivial. On the contrary, the question loomed large in all our minds. Children could be devastatingly honest critics, and the wrong person playing the part could ruin the occasion for everyone. At last we all felt satisfied the matter was settled, even though Norman knew nothing about it. Talking about Norman reminded me that I had agreed to do a two week stint at the village grocery store while the newlyweds were away.

Hannah had assured me she was all set up to cope without me. Michelle was keen to earn some extra cash for Christmas, and she would be covering my morning shifts; Cliff had said he could manage at the pub without her until lunchtime. Toby and Michelle had met because she worked as his mother's carer. She lived close to the pub and the tea shop, meaning Naomi could call Michelle if she needed her, while Michelle was out at work. Hannah's mother was also happy to help out at the tea shop if Hannah was struggling to cope on her own. So, everything was settled. Only now the time had arrived, I wasn't feeling as relaxed about the situation as when we had first made all the arrangements.

'It's only for two weeks,' Hannah had reassured me. 'But I'm glad you'll be back before the Christmas rush. There's no way I could manage without you once it gets manic. We've already had tons of bookings. It's going to be a nightmare,' she added cheerfully.

It was late by the time we left the pub, and Hannah, Adam and I walked back down the High Street together, with Poppy either straining at her lead wanting to run on ahead, or stopping to sniff at the ground. As we waited for Hannah to store the excess food in the tea shop, Adam and I discussed the empty premises over the road from Hannah's café. A notice announced it had been let. The windows had been painted white, indicating that something was going on inside, but the only other sign so far merely announced, in flowery letters, 'Opening in time for Christmas!' None of us knew who had rented it. I thought it was exciting, not knowing what was coming, but Hannah was anxious.

We reached the top of my lane, where Hannah and Adam said goodbye to me and walked on towards their little house across the river. From the top of my road it was only a short way down Mill Lane to Rosecroft. Had I been on my own, it would have taken me two minutes to walk past the one other property in the lane where Adam's father, Richard, lived. With Poppy, it took longer, as she insisted on stopping to sniff every inch of the grass verge. At last we reached our cottage and settled down for the night. It had been a busy day.

3

ON MONDAY, I WAS due to start working at Maud's shop, the local grocery store which was rather grandly named the Village Emporium. To be fair to Maud and the pretentious name she had given her shop, it was larger than it appeared from the front as the interior went back a surprisingly long way. The shop was packed with shelves from floor to ceiling, crammed with all manner of tins and packets, household items and cleaning materials. In short, it was a veritable Aladdin's Cave containing everything anyone could possibly need in order to survive, were the villagers ever to find themselves isolated from the outside world. While Swindon, with its vast supermarkets, was not far away, going there involved a journey by car or bus, and a round trip could take as much as an hour in travelling time alone. But Maud's main competitors were Amazon and online deliveries from supermarkets, which she hated with a passion. Her tiny figure seemed to seize up and her fists clenched whenever internet shopping was mentioned.

Aware that she couldn't hope to compete with other suppliers on price, she offered weekly Bargain Buys and

Special Offers, as a means of attracting customers into her shop. She also had a singular advantage over any other outlet: her seemingly endless supply of local gossip. No one could expect a baby, or lose their job, or be fined for a minor traffic offence, without Maud knowing about it. She seemed to absorb local news from the ether. Her relentless prying wasn't driven solely by curiosity. Gossip and rumour were the fuel that ensured the survival of her business. Even the local paper couldn't vie with Maud for local information, and she was careful never to share her secrets with anyone other than her numerous customers. People went to the Village Emporium ostensibly to shop, but more often than not they were only there to hear the latest news, and Maud rarely disappointed. Having made a purchase, customers went away agog with the latest local scandal about who had fallen out with a neighbour over an overgrown tree, or who was suspected of embarking on a clandestine liaison, and Maud just kept on counting up her takings at the end of the day.

Since it was my first day in what promised to be a challenging job, I was up early to take Poppy to Jane's house where she would be spending the day with Hannah's mother and her placid old dog, Holly. To begin with, Holly had found Poppy's puppyish antics tiresome. While Poppy had darted around, barking, in a frantic attempt to attract the old dog's attention, Holly had closed her eyes and ignored her younger companion's efforts to win her over. Eventually persuaded that Holly did not want to play with her, Poppy had settled down and contented herself with the old dog's quiet companionship. No longer a puppy, Poppy was now more staid than she had been when she first met Holly. So, after a shaky start, the two dogs had become firm friends. With Poppy taken care of during the day, I was free to concentrate on my new responsibilities.

To my relief, Hannah had refused to leave me on my own in the café until I had been working there for some months and was confident about coping on my own. Although we only offered food and drinks from a relatively limited menu, everything we served was homemade and most of the food was freshly baked. To ensure we never ran short, Hannah kept back-up provisions in the freezer, with everything frozen while fresh from the oven, and put in the oven straight from the freezer. When the tea shop was not busy, Hannah would be occupied filling the freezer. With Hannah responsible for the baking, all I had to do was make sure we had enough milk, heat up bread and pastries in the microwave, brew pots of tea, and serve customers. We were busy, but the job was not complicated.

Working in Maud's shop posed very different challenges. In addition to serving customers, Maud had evolved her own idiosyncratic systems for recording transactions, and for reordering supplies when they were running low. She kept a handwritten note of every purchase and every sale in a large red ledger, where her minute scrawl was almost indecipherable, even with a magnifying glass. To make matters worse, with the approach of Christmas, there were a host of unusual orders flooding in, which she identified with unintelligible symbols.

'Can't people here just use Amazon like everyone else in the world?' I grumbled to Maud's nephew, Barry, the local policeman, who had taken the morning off to help me.

I should have thanked Barry when he told me he didn't want me to worry, and he would help me as much and as often as he possibly could. His eagerness to help me was reassuring yet, at the same time, unnerving. Although he made no secret of his fondness for me, Barry's offer to help had been motivated more by loyalty to Maud than concern for me. Barry was gentle and decent, steady and reliable, in fact exactly the kind of man of whom my mother would approve. He had asked me out several times, eventually giving up when it became clear that we were never likely to become romantically involved. Although I had nothing against him, I wasn't attracted to him and had never encouraged him, but despite my repeated rejection of his advances, we had never fallen out. He had assured me he was a patient man, and I had given up trying to persuade him that we were never going to end up together. So we had established a friendship based on mutual acceptance of each other's sentiments. Now I felt ambivalent towards him, hoping he would not try to exploit the fact that I was floundering in the grocery store. Seeing how I needed his support, I was afraid he might try to take advantage of my situation and resume his efforts to win me round. Resolved never to encourage him, I was equally determined not to let Maud down, so was cautiously pleased to accept his help.

It was easy for Norman's regular assistant, Billy, to manage the butcher's in Norman's absence. Billy had been working there for several years and was familiar with the set-up, whereas I had never worked in a shop, let alone been left in sole charge of one. Where I struggled to make sense of Maud's records, Barry read them easily. Sales were of little interest to me personally; the revenue was not mine. Maud would have to square the takings with the sales on her return. But I needed to keep the village shop properly stocked or risk losing Maud her customers. Once consumers turned to alternative suppliers, they rarely returned to the more expensive local shop. So I couldn't afford to let the Village Emporium run out of anything. Apart from the threat posed by online monoliths, Swindon was not far away, with its multiple outlets: supermarkets and bricks and mortar shops of all sizes, stocking whatever people might want to buy. Barry was keen to help me, but even he wasn't sure how Christmas usually affected his aunt's orders. Meanwhile, time was fast running out for last minute reordering. Leafing through Maud's previous year's ledger, I was struggling to compare sales from last Christmas with our current position, when we received the first delivery of the week. Barry had to leave, so I set to work unpacking the crates by myself. It was strenuous work. Clearly Maud was stronger than she looked.

The stock room rapidly descended into chaos as I tried to sort newly delivered items into some kind of logical order, piling them up so that tins were with similar tins, packets of cereal were together, and so on. Without warning, a tower of precariously stacked soup tins toppled over, crushing a pile of bags of crisps and nuts, the impact of that collapse causing packets of cereal to knock over a collection of piled up plastic tubs of washing powder which landed on a selection of Christmas decorations. Baubles of every colour burst out of a cellophane bag and rolled around other jumbled items. Setting out to retrieve the bright glass balls, which thankfully hadn't broken, I tripped over a broom handle and lost my footing. Luckily for me, some packs of toilet rolls broke my fall. I was only slightly bruised, but some of the toilet paper wrappers were torn and the toilet rolls themselves were squashed. There was no time to sort through the shambles to see what had been delivered before customers began to arrive.

The first customer asked for oranges. Although listed on the delivery note, they were not to be found. I searched through the whole consignment of newly arrived items, but there was no sign of them. The same happened with the next customer, who came in asking for apples. At this point, I had to acknowledge that none of the fruit on Maud's order had turned up, although it was all listed on the delivery note. After failing to persuade disappointed customers to buy tinned peaches of which, for some reason, we had several dozen cans, I phoned the supplier to find out when we might expect the remainder of the order. And that was just the start of my problems. The missing fruit was not my fault, but the spilt milk was entirely down to me. At least one customer left, grumbling impatiently, while I mopped up milk and swept broken glass, using a new mop and broom which were the only ones I could find. Maud's profits for the day were slowly being eroded in front of my eyes, not to mention the goodwill I was losing among her regular customers.

At about half past three, a gang of children charged into the shop in mud-stained coats with torn pockets and hanging hems. Exuberant at being let out of school, they seized chocolate bars and packets of sweets in their grimy fists, and thrust coins at me in quick-fire succession. Jumping around excitedly while I fiddled with their change, they managed to knock over a stack of cereal boxes, one of which split open, spilling rice crispies all over the floor. When I told the children they would have to pay for the waste, they burst out in a shrill chorus, blaming each other for what had happened.

'I'm not paying. It wasn't my fault,' they each claimed indignantly.

Eventually, they reached a consensus, and accused me of having caused the accident.

'How could I have knocked it over?' I protested. 'I was here behind the counter the whole time.'

'You was too slow,' the ringleader explained. 'You kept us waiting too long. It's bound to happen if you keep us hanging around like that. What are we supposed to do?'

'In any case, we got no more money,' another grubby little boy announced.

At this rate, my wages for the day would be spent on a list of unwanted purchases: Christmas decorations, milk, mop, broom and toilet rolls, not to mention other items which were now unusable, like spilt milk and rice crispies. It was a depressing thought. I wasn't sure how I got through the remainder of the day but at last I closed the door and reckoned up the day's takings. To my surprise, we hadn't done badly, despite having lurched from one disaster to another. Having paid for the losses, I took the mop, broom and squashed toilet rolls home with me. They were still usable and there was no point in throwing them away. After my chaotic first day, I was late collecting Poppy from Jane. Poppy was excited to see me, as she always was when we had been apart. Jane didn't mind that I was late, and enquired kindly how my day had gone. Too tired and dispirited to go into any detail, I merely replied that everything was fine. It must have been obvious that wasn't true, but she didn't challenge my claim.

I stopped at the Sunshine Tea Shoppe on my way home and found Hannah was still there, baking for the next day. We sat down for a quick chat. By the time I had downed a couple of cups of tea and polished off two of Hannah's scones that really did seem to melt in the mouth, I realised that my day hadn't gone so badly after all. At least I had survived, and the shop was still standing. When Hannah reassured me that Maud's customers would remain loyal, if only to hear her gossip, I felt a lot better.

'I just don't want to let her down,' I said.

'How did it go with Barry?' Hannah asked.

I shrugged. Hannah knew all about Barry's interest in me, and about my feelings towards him. She claimed to understand how I felt, but I wasn't sure she really did.

'He's really nice, and you know how much he likes you,' she had said more than once. 'I can't see why you wouldn't want to go out with him. You could at least give him a chance.'

'I did go out for supper with him once,' I protested, but Hannah dismissed my halfhearted claim.

'That's not what I'm talking about,' she said.

In a way, she had a point. The trouble was, Barry was a friend. If we went out together and broke up, the result could be devastating if it was even slightly acrimonious. At the very least it might be disappointing for one or both of us, and then my circle of friends might be split. I was good friends with Hannah and Toby, but they had both known Barry since they were children starting school together.

They had only known me for three years. It was unlikely either of them would choose me over Barry, particularly if he was the injured party, as seemed a likely outcome if we went out together. The cost would be too high if things didn't work out between us. When I explained my thinking, Hannah had to concede it sounded sensible. But the way she uttered the word 'sensible' somehow made it sound like a criticism. We chatted for a short while about Barry, and Adam, and Christmas, until it was time for her to take her scones and buns out of the oven and go home. She told me Adam had helped her for a few hours.

'So that's me out of a job then?' I replied.

She shook her head, laughing. 'Honestly, Emily, he's hopeless. We've already had a lot of bookings for Christmas week and I'm really going to need you here. Maud had better not be delayed or I don't know how I'll manage.' She turned to look at me and spoke earnestly. 'The tea shop will be your priority, won't it, once your two weeks are up? To be honest, I'm sorry I ever agreed to let you help Maud out. I've had to stay late because I don't have time to bake and serve at the same time. We've been busy here all day. I thought it would be easy enough to carry on without you for a couple of weeks, with Michelle and mum helping out, but I don't know how I used to manage without you.'

A warm feeling spread through me, on hearing my friend needed me, and I couldn't help smiling.

'Well?' she prompted me. 'Do I have your word you'll be back as soon as Maud returns? I need to know.'

Quickly I reassured her that I would definitely be back working in the tea shop after two weeks, even if Maud didn't return on time.

'This is my job,' I told her. 'And more than that, you are my best friend.'

It was Hannah's turn to smile. She stood up and held out her arms to hug me. Held in her warm embrace, I was more convinced than ever that it would be mad to risk losing her friendship by going out with Barry.

4

THE NEXT MORNING, THE weather was quite mild for November. Two customers came into the shop chattering volubly. One was a woman with short white hair, while her companion had artificially black hair that was probably dyed, but looked like a wig. I recognised them from their visits to the Sunshine Tea Shoppe where they came every Wednesday at eleven o'clock on the dot for two cups of tea and two fruit scones. It wasn't an expensive order, but regular customers helped the tea shop survive during quiet times. Over the spring and summer, tourists passing through our picturesque village gave Hannah a significant boost to her profits, but during the colder months she depended on local residents to keep her going. That morning, in Maud's shop, I overheard one of them mention Hannah's name. After that, I couldn't help trying to listen to their conversation.

'Hannah's not going to be best pleased,' the white-haired woman said, shaking her head.

'It's going to give her a real headache,' the dark-haired woman agreed gravely.

'It'll be a thorn in her side all right,' the other woman went on.

'French as well, by all accounts. Ooh la la,' her companion said in a comical voice, rolling her eyes, and they both laughed.

'Well, I feel sorry for Hannah,' the first woman said, growing serious again. 'It's no laughing matter for her. Something like this is bound to knock her for six.'

'It's a shame for her, but what can you do? It's a jungle out there.'

'Even in Ashton Mead.'

They both sighed. While I was puzzling over what they meant, they wandered out of earshot, still talking. Their heads bobbed up and down as they nattered, but I could no longer hear what they were saying. I was considering following them on some pretext or other, when another customer approached the counter carrying a full basket, and I couldn't leave my post at the till. After that, I was busy for the rest of the day. Occasionally there was a lull in customers for a few moments, allowing me to investigate the morning's delivery. Without knowing where some items were displayed, I often had to resort to guesswork in refilling the shelves. It was never long before my efforts to empty the crates were interrupted. I was puzzling over where to put some jars of pickles when a flurry of people arrived at the same time. What with serving customers and stacking shelves, there was no time to speculate about what might have happened to threaten Hannah's happiness.

It was impossible to take a break, so I gobbled down an egg sandwich at two o'clock and even then I was interrupted by a customer who was waiting to pay. Bolting my sandwich so quickly gave me hiccups that lasted for ages. It had never before occurred to me to wonder how Maud ran the shop singlehanded with such apparent ease. Perhaps she had nibbled energy bars in the few quiet moments between customers. She had lived above the shop, before her marriage, so probably spent time filling the shelves in the evenings, or early in the morning before she opened the doors to customers. Keen to fetch Poppy as soon as I could, I could only stay in the shop during opening hours.

During the afternoon, I overheard Hannah's name mentioned again in snippets of conversation.

'Hannah must be worried,' an old lady mumbled, as she paused to check her change.

'Worried?' I repeated, genuinely puzzled and a little apprehensive. 'Why would she be worried?'

The old woman tapped the side of her nose with a knobbly finger and turned away without answering. Shortly after that, an old man asked me outright what Hannah was going to do about it. His wife, who was standing at his side, watched me closely, as though searching my face for clues that would resolve some mystery.

'Do about what?' I asked. 'I'm sorry, but I don't know what you're talking about. She isn't planning on making any changes, as far as I'm aware.'

The woman nodded thoughtfully. 'That's probably the most sensible approach,' she agreed. 'I dare say it won't last long. There's no point in her getting her knickers in a twist over it.'

I still had no idea what they were talking about. Before I could question them, another customer wanted to know where the pickles were, and I was distracted by having to hunt for the jars I knew I had placed on a shelf that morning. By the time we tracked them down, the old couple had gone and it was too late to ask them about Hannah.

Not until I was on my way home with Poppy that evening, did I learn the reason for the gossip about Hannah. Walking down the High Street to see if she was still in the tea shop baking, I discovered the identity of the tenant who was renting the property across the road from us. On a shiny pink background, the words *Patisserie Desirée* were emblazoned in ornate gold letters. I let out an involuntary cry on learning that a French patisserie was opening directly over the road from the Sunshine Tea Shoppe. No wonder villagers were speculating about the adverse effect this might have on Hannah's business. The tea shop was closed for the day and there were no lights on. Nervously, I crossed the road and stood outside the new patisserie. As Poppy sniffed at the pavement and cocked her leg, I studied the place from the outside. It looked inviting, with a large sign in the window announcing the offer of a special '*Fête de Noël*' menu with half price '*Patisseries Françaises Authentiques*'. It didn't take a French speaker to understand what that meant. It was scant consolation to know that Poppy had peed against the wall of the new cake shop.

That evening I met up with Hannah and Adam in the pub. Like her customers who had visited the grocery shop, Hannah was talking about the patisserie that was shortly to open in the village. She was understandably afraid that such competition right on her doorstep would threaten the survival of the business she had worked so hard to establish.

'English scones or French pastries?' she asked wretchedly. 'That's what everyone's talking about, isn't it? And it's only going to take a few of my regulars to defect across the road, and we'll be ruined.' She sighed. 'We'll be completely ruined. I just don't see how we can survive.'

Adam and I did our best to reassure her that the French pastries couldn't be authentic, and in any case a so-called French patisserie couldn't possibly compete with her tea shop with its freshly baked homemade scones and cakes. Hannah remained quietly distraught, convinced that her enterprise was as good as finished. Her apprehension was understandable. Having ploughed all the money from her generous divorce settlement into the Sunshine Tea Shoppe, she had worked hard for years to build a loyal customer base. It would be heartbreaking to see the results of her efforts slip away, and all because a rival café had opened right on her doorstep.

'Why did they have to open here, in the village?' she asked. 'Ashton Mead doesn't need another café. And why do they have to park themselves right in the middle of the High Street, directly opposite my tea shop? Couldn't they find somewhere else? How many villages are there round here? Why did they have to choose Ashton Mead?'

There was no answer to her questions, other than to say that sometimes bad luck struck for no reason. But that wasn't helpful. I felt doubly guilty about leaving to go and work for Maud, even temporarily, knowing Hannah was struggling alone. Adam remained resolutely optimistic, declaring he was convinced that *Patisserie Desirée* wouldn't last long. He insisted that many new cafés and restaurants failed to stay open for long.

'Anyone can conjure up a few pastries, but you know better than anyone that it takes a lot more than fancy baking to run a successful business. And if they're selling their stuff at half price, that might attract customers in the short term, but they won't manage to make ends meet,' he assured her cheerily. 'We just have to be patient. As soon as they hike their prices up, people will stop going there. They'll be gone soon enough, you'll see.'

Hannah looked at him miserably. 'You can't know that. And in the meantime, what about the Christmas period? This couldn't have come at a worse time. We always stay open for longer over Christmas because we're usually so busy.'

'You've had lots of bookings –' I began but she interrupted me.

'Some of them have cancelled,' she muttered, almost in tears. 'And who knows if the others will even turn up?'

I had never seen my friend looking so downhearted before. Even when she had fallen out with Adam, she had managed to remain optimistic. Her usual response to problems was to throw a party, but this time even the prospect of Christmas failed to lift her spirits. Seeing her so forlorn, I wished there was something I could do to help, but I was stuck at Maud's shop for the next week and a half, and couldn't even support Hannah by serving more efficiently and being more welcoming to customers in the Sunshine Tea Shoppe. As for Adam, he was fully occupied with his own work and unable to take any more time off, other than during his lunch hour. I felt wretched knowing that my best friend was in trouble and I could do nothing to help her.

It didn't improve Hannah's mood when we overheard an elderly couple on the next table talking about the new patisserie. Like the women in the shop that morning, I recognised them as regular customers of the tea shop. No doubt Hannah did too. The chances were they would try the patisserie once and then return to Hannah's tea shop, but there was no guarantee of that. If the French pastries were as alluring as its sparkling new signage, Hannah might lose many of her regular customers.

'And she said the menu's all written in French,' the woman was saying.

'How are we supposed to know what to order if it's all in French? I hope you can speak French, because I certainly can't.'

'Well, they'll have to tell us what everything is, if we ask them,' the woman replied. 'We might even learn a bit of French. You never know, it could be useful.'

'How is being able to order a cupcake in French going to be of any use to you?' the man asked her, laughing.

We didn't hear her answer.

'Having the patisserie over the road might not be a bad thing,' I told Hannah, in an attempt to look on the bright side. 'If they attract new customers to the High Street, some of them might come to us as well.'

Hannah laughed bitterly. 'This is Ashton Mead,' she said, 'not London. How many people are likely to go out for tea and cakes? There are barely enough customers to keep us afloat as it is. There aren't going to be enough to support two cafés, virtually next door to one another.'

'Tourists will still want to visit a traditional English tea shop,' I pointed out.

But we both knew that the opening of a rival facility right on our doorstep was bound to put a dent in Hannah's takings, and her profits were already slim. A blow like this might ruin her business for good. Adam and I gazed helplessly at one another. There was nothing we could say.

Just then Cliff came over to collect empty glasses. 'So, who's going to try out this new patisserie?' he asked jovially and stopped, as I gave a barely perceptible shake of my head. Registering Hannah's fraught expression, he frowned.

As though sensing tension around the table, Poppy whimpered.

'I was thinking I might give it a go, just out of curiosity,' Cliff went on, with a show of diffidence. 'But it won't be a patch on a proper English tea shop, take it from me. Give me Hannah's scones over fancy French pastries any day.'

Poppy jumped up and wagged her tail before going over to Hannah and laying her chin on my friend's feet. But even Poppy couldn't cheer Hannah up for long.

'We can't sit here spending money all evening,' she said bitterly.

Adam mumbled under his breath about overreacting, but she put her coat on and made for the door and he hurried after her, calling out a hurried goodnight as they left.

5

IN MANY WAYS, MY second week in Maud's shop was less challenging than the first week had been, as I became familiar with the routine and learned where different items were displayed. Since there seemed to be no logic to the way Maud arranged her stock, it was a case of memorising the layout. Had I been in charge permanently, things might have been different, but it wasn't my place to start making alterations. I had survived my first week more or less intact and had only to keep the shop ticking over for another week until Maud returned. Poppy's routine hadn't altered much with the change in my work pattern, so at least I didn't have to worry about her. When we arrived at Jane's house early every morning, Poppy would trot over to lie down companionably beside Holly who would raise an ear and wag her tail gently. I wondered how Poppy would react when she visited Jane and found Holly was no longer there.

'Will you get another dog when Holly isn't here anymore?' I asked Jane one day.

She shook her head. 'I hope that's a long way off yet,' she said, unwilling to talk about losing her old dog.

I looked down at Poppy, frisking at my feet, and felt a pang of inexpressible sadness, knowing her life expectancy was short compared to mine.

'Yes,' I agreed. 'I'm sure she'll be here for a long time to come.'

Jane smiled in appreciation of my fib. 'I'll deal with it when the time comes,' she added softly, stroking her Holly's back.

Holly didn't open her eyes, but her tail thumped gently on the floor, and for a second I felt like crying.

Even starting my day early, there still wasn't enough time to do everything that needed to be done during my working hours at the shop. It was physically wearing as well as stressful, and I couldn't wait for Maud to return. My admiration for her stamina grew to something like awe. One afternoon Barry confirmed what I had already suspected, that Maud used to spend her evenings checking stock and working out her orders. We both wondered how her attitude might change now she was no longer living alone. Barry told me that he had tried to persuade her to modernise her till, so it would register details of each individual item sold as well as how much money was taken. There were computer systems, he'd explained, that automatically recorded stock levels of each commodity and flagged up when anything was running low. They made reordering a doddle, he said, because stock levels would be updated electronically for her as she went along. His aunt insisted she preferred to stick to her own antiquated way of working, which involved keeping a handwritten record of every transaction. When he pressed her, she insisted that she was too old to change her habits.

'She won't listen,' he said. 'I know some older people find technology challenging, but I could help her, if she'd only be a bit more open minded about it.'

'Perhaps Norman will change her mind,' I suggested. 'I don't suppose he'll want her to be working in the shop every evening.'

I wouldn't have been able to manage the shop by myself, but Barry turned up every day shortly before closing time to help me check what we needed to order, and to deal with Maud's suppliers. While grateful for his help, I was uncomfortable being in his debt, but I had no choice if I was going to cope with the shop in Maud's absence. If her return was delayed, I told him he would have to manage without me, or the grocery shop would have to close until she was back. I had promised to resume my duties at the tea shop after two weeks. Barry laughed and told me the village shop never closed.

'There's always a first time,' I warned him. 'Don't count your chickens.'

Barry flinched as though he had been stung. 'Chickens,' he cried out, slapping the side of his head. 'I almost forgot. We need to order some frozen chicken thighs. Old Mrs Delaney will be in for them at the end of the week.'

During the day, Barry left me on my own at the till. Card payments were relatively straightforward as long as the card reader worked. It occasionally played up, and of course that only happened when Barry wasn't around to sort it out for me. Some old ladies still preferred to pay in cash, and it was a challenge to give them the right change on the spot. By keeping a small notebook and pen by the till, I was able to jot down my sums and that helped speed up the process. As the end of the fortnight approached, I became quite adept at manning the till. Replenishing stock remained a challenge and it was a constant struggle to stay on top of things. I was reminding myself that Maud was due back soon, and smiling through my agitation, when a stranger entered the shop and distracted me from my scribbled sums. Flustered, I gave old Miss Frobisher the incorrect change. Fortunately, she was more alert than me -and honest- or the till would have been three pounds short at the end of the day.

The stranger was tall and slender, with sandy-coloured hair cut very short at the back and longer on the top of his head. He was wearing a tight-fitting navy jumper and jeans. For an instant his gaze held mine. Staring into his startlingly bright blue eyes, I was aware that he was smiling straight at me, and felt a flicker of attraction which I hoped was mutual. There was something irresistible about his smile. He appeared to be about my own age. He turned away, and I was drawn back to Miss Frobisher's tutting. The stranger and I had only exchanged one brief glance, but in that instant I had felt a kind of magnetic attraction between us. Wondering whether he felt the same way, I imagined our feelings developing into something deeper than a passing attraction. A few minutes later, he joined the short queue to pay and I was able to study him covertly as I operated the card reader, doing my best to appear efficient, and fumbling hopelessly with the keys. A quick glance at the man's hands revealed that he wasn't wearing a wedding ring. That was no guarantee he was single, of course, but I felt optimistic.

*

'I asked for a receipt,' a customer said tartly. Momentarily distracted, I had forgotten to press the right button on the card reader. I imagined the stranger vaulting over the counter to assist me and smiled involuntarily, which irritated the customer further. I apologised and assured her Maud would be back the following week and she went off, slightly mollified but still grumbling at my ineptitude. The stranger approached with a full basket, which I thought would please Maud, but I was startled on seeing what he was buying. He had packed his basket with what looked like almost all our bags of flour, and our entire stock of butter and raisins and cooking chocolate.

'That's a lot of butter,' I murmured stupidly, wondering how other customers were going to react if we ran out of such a basic product. Apart from anything else, I knew Hannah was going to need some, but hadn't got round to putting a few packets aside for her yet. Staring at his purchases, I was forced to choose between failing Hannah, by not saving her any butter, or Maud, by turning away a new customer who wanted to spend money in her shop. When he smiled at me, I felt a flutter of excitement so strong it made me shiver. In that moment, I would have sold him the entire contents of the shop just to detain him. Ringing up everything in his basket, I lowered my gaze and read the name on his credit card: C. Winters. I wanted to ask him what the C stood for, but was suddenly reticent.

'I haven't seen you in here before,' I said brightly, forcing myself to meet his gaze and hoping I wouldn't blush. 'But that's probably because I don't normally work here. I'm just helping out temporarily while the owner is away. Do you know the owner, Maud? I usually work at the Sunshine Tea Shoppe in the High Street. Maybe you've seen it?'

Aware that I was babbling foolishly, I hoped he wouldn't see through my clumsy attempt to let him know where to find me again. My face felt hot. Afraid that my cheeks had turned bright red with embarrassment, I fixed my eyes on the till.

'Do you live in the village?' he enquired politely.

With a nod, I told him I had been there for three years. 'You'll find we're very friendly here,' I added, looking up and giving him an encouraging smile.

'So, I suppose you moved here because you married a local man?' he asked.

'No,' I replied. 'I'm single. That is,' I added quickly, in case he had the impression I wasn't interested in men, 'I had a boyfriend, but we split up. I moved here because –'

On the point of telling him about my great aunt's bequest, I hesitated. The stranger's question about my relationship status implied that he found me attractive. If that was the case, I wanted to know he was interested in me for my own sake, before telling him that I owned my own home, mortgage free. It was an enviable position for a woman in her twenties. Having dumped me, my previous boyfriend had tried to get back together with me as soon as he learned about my inheritance. It had taken me a while to see through his duplicity, and the experience had made me wary of men who flirted with me. Not that men were exactly queuing up to ask me out. In fact, apart from Toby and Barry, no one had expressed even a passing interest in me romantically since my painful break up with my ex. But I was still afraid my mortgage-free property might attract another man to pursue me for the wrong reasons.

Just then, a local woman, Marjorie, entered the shop. She stared inquisitively at the stranger as he finished packing his purchases into a couple of carrier bags. As a rule, the only unfamiliar faces we saw in Maud's grocery store were those of people stopping on their way to somewhere else. This man didn't give the impression he was just passing through the village. With a parting smile and a friendly wave he left, whistling cheerily, leaving me to wonder who he was and whether he had really come to live in the village.

'Who was that?' Marjorie asked me. 'What's he doing in Ashton Mead? I haven't seen him here before. Does he live in the village? How long has he been here?'

On hearing that I didn't know anything about the stranger, she frowned at me as though I had disappointed her. I understood why. Maud would have quizzed the intriguing newcomer shamelessly to find out his name, where he had come from, what he was doing in the village, and how long he intended to stay. But I wasn't Maud and, to be fair, few people could boast her talent for wheedling information out of customers in order to spread the latest tittle-tattle.

'I suppose he works at the new patisserie in the High Street,' Marjorie said with a disapproving sniff.

It wasn't clear if her disdain was directed at me for my failure to extract any information from the newcomer, or at the new café for setting up in competition with Hannah, or for some other reason known only to herself. In Maud's absence, rumours about the new patisserie were rife, but no one was able to confirm any of the stories. All we knew for certain was that it would be opening soon in time for Christmas. The shop door being close to the till, I often overheard snippets of conversation when two or more people entered together, and the new patisserie was on everyone's lips.

'I'm telling you, I saw her with my own eyes,' a villager was saying to her friend later that day as they walked into the shop. They were both quite young, and were pushing strollers with babies in them.

'So what's she like?' the taller of the two women asked. 'I heard she's French.'

'I don't know about that, but I'm almost sure she was the proprietor of that la-de-da new café. At least I think she must have been the proprietor. She could have been the manager. She seemed to be in charge anyway.'

'What's she like?' her companion enquired again.

That was a question I wanted to ask, and I listened carefully to the description of Hannah's business rival. According to the villager who had witnessed the scene, a smartly dressed blonde woman had been complaining about the gold lettering of the new sign above the entrance to the patisserie. A man in white overalls appeared to be remonstrating with her, but the woman describing the incident had not been able to hear what they were saying.

'She sounds a bit of a diva,' the tall woman said. 'How old is she?'

'It's difficult to say. I was on the other side of the road, and only caught sight of her for a few seconds. That Christmas tree was in the way and, in any case, I didn't like to peer at her too obviously. Then Jason started yelling, and I walked on. She didn't look round. She seemed too engrossed in her conversation to notice us.'

I listened attentively to the exchange, until the two women moved away. Whatever the French woman was like, her arrival in Ashton Mead didn't bode well for the Sunshine Tea Shoppe. I felt a cold shiver run down my back as I thought of my friend and what she stood to lose.

6

WORRIED ABOUT UPSETTING HANNAH, I resolved not to refer to her competitor in her presence. As it turned out, it was impossible to avoid the topic that evening in the pub. Not having seen Poppy all day, I was happy to make a fuss of her without talking about anything much, when Hannah herself brought up the subject of the new patisserie. She too had observed the altercation mentioned by one of Maud's customers. As soon as Hannah mentioned it, Adam, Toby and I leaned forward, keen to hear more, as though we had all been deliberately holding back from speaking about it until then. Even Poppy rolled over and sat up, putting her head on one side as though listening attentively to what Hannah had to say.

'I'm guessing the woman I saw was the owner,' Hannah told us. 'At any rate, she seemed to be bossing everyone around.'

'Who was she bossing around?' Adam asked.

'What difference does it make?' Hannah replied. 'If you must know, there was a man putting up a great big sign outside.'

'So this "everyone" you're talking about was one tradesman,' Adam said, with a teasing smirk.

Hannah rebuked him for being pedantic, and he complained that she needed to be more accurate in her reporting.

'So was she the owner?' I asked, interrupting their banter.

'Well, she was certainly strutting about as though she owned the place,' Hannah said. 'And I can only describe the sign as vulgar. It certainly doesn't match the style of the other shops along the High Street. It's a real "look at me" sign, you know what I mean? Just loud and brash. It wouldn't look out of place in Las Vegas, or outside a night club in London, but it doesn't look right in Ashton Mead.'

Adam laughed at her. 'When did you last go to a night club in London?'

'You'd be surprised what I used to get up to before I met you,' she replied archly.

Now that the subject of the patisserie had been raised, I was curious to hear more about the owner. The customer in Maud's shop had been frustratingly vague, but I suspected Hannah would have studied her competitor closely.

'From what I could see, she was heavily made up,' Hannah said. 'It was difficult to tell from across the street, but it looked like she was wearing false eyelashes. She had a kind of bouffant hairstyle, like those high hats worn by sentries outside Buckingham Palace, only blonde. You know the ones I mean?'

'So you're saying she looks like a haystack?' Adam suggested.

'Well, kind of, only I suppose she was more elegant than that. She was wearing a bright pink coat and teetered about on high heels as though she was at a fashion show.'

Adam frowned. 'Not like a haystack, then?'

'Anyway, the whole outfit looked totally impractical, in my opinion,' Hannah said, ignoring Adam's interjection. 'And if she thinks she's going to be on her feet all day in those stiletto heels…'

With a grimace, Hannah shook her head and took a gulp of her pint before adding that she didn't think the French woman and her patisserie were going to fit in with village life. I suspected that was wishful thinking on Hannah's part, but made no comment. Hannah launched into a description of the sign which, she claimed, outdid the Christmas tree in brilliance, in her opinion. While we were talking, Toby went to the bar for another round and stood there chatting for a while to his girlfriend, the barmaid. I liked Michelle, although she had always been very reserved with me. She probably knew that Toby and I had enjoyed a close friendship before he met her. We had never been anything more than good friends, but I had once dallied with the prospect of a romantic relationship with him, and Toby had intimated that he felt the same way. For a time I had waited for him to speak, but nothing even vaguely intimate had ever happened between us. I had suspected he was holding back because his mother took up a lot of his time. Naomi had several carers, but Toby was her only child and he liked to keep an eye on her to make sure she was well looked after.

Once Michelle and Toby started seeing each other, I dismissed my chagrin and I don't think anyone realised how miffed I felt. Hannah had been egging me on to go out with Toby, but even she seemed oblivious to my dismay. Concealed from everyone, my disappointment soon faded. Toby was a good friend, and I was content to see him happy with someone else.

Hannah brightened up when I reminded her that Maud was due back the next day, meaning I would be able to turn up for work at the Sunshine Tea Shoppe first thing in the morning.

'I can't wait for you to come back,' she smiled. 'It's been heavy going without you. No one to share a pot of tea with before opening the door in the morning, and no one to chat with at the end of the day. I've really missed you.'

'I've missed you too,' I admitted. 'At least you had Michelle and your mum to keep you company.'

'And you had Barry,' she replied, and we both laughed.

It was true that, like Hannah, I had been missing our regular chats. Neither of us mentioned that the patisserie would be opening its doors imminently, but the thought of it loomed over us like a dark cloud threatening to obscure the sun. Toby returned from the bar and the conversation moved on to everyone's plans for Christmas. Hannah protested when Toby told us he and Michelle were planning to stay with her parents in the North of England.

'Why don't her parents come to us?' Hannah suggested. 'We've got plenty of room at the tea shop. Adam's father and brother and his family, and my mother, and Emily's parents and her sister and her family are all coming, along with a few locals I've invited who were going to be on their own. There's going to be quite a party of us already. We've got plenty of room, and a few more will be welcome.

And it works for Naomi for you to come to us,' she added pointedly, referring to Toby's mother. 'I don't suppose Michelle's parents can accommodate her overnight, and she'll want to spend Christmas with you and Michelle, won't she?'

We all knew better than to try and change Hannah's mind once she had decided to throw a party. A natural hostess, she loved cooking for as many guests as possible. If the Sunshine Tea Shoppe ever closed down, I was sure she could start a successful business catering for wedding parties. I had suggested that to her once, but she had snapped at me that she was perfectly happy with her existing business. I hadn't liked to mention it again, in case she thought I had no faith the tea shop would survive.

'You must all come to us,' Hannah repeated to Toby. 'I'm going to cater for you anyway, so if you don't come, there'll be tons of food going to waste and it will be all your fault.'

Toby shook his head. 'I don't think it's practical. For a start, Michelle's got a sister,' he began.

'We've got plenty of room,' Hannah repeated doggedly.

'And two nieces and a grandmother,' he added.

'The more the merrier,' Hannah insisted. 'Seriously, how many of them can there be? You know we have plenty of room at the tea shop. And we've got a toilet that Naomi can use, so it makes perfect sense for us to host. I really want everyone to come to me,' she added, her voice becoming plaintive. 'This might be the last year I'm able to host a party like this. Next year Adam and I might be forced to have a small Christmas lunch at home, with only room for the two of us, if the tea shop has to close.'

It wasn't clear if she was seriously worried, or trying to guilt trip Toby into agreeing to her plans, but he shrugged and promised he would talk to Michelle about it.

'We'll chip in, if we do come,' he added, looking slightly uneasy. 'There could be quite a few of us.'

'Me too,' I piped up quickly. 'I don't expect you to stump up for a Christmas dinner for all my family.'

Hannah nodded. 'We'll work something out,' she said, waving her hand vaguely. 'So, that's settled then. Everyone is coming to the tea shop for Christmas lunch.'

Toby thanked her for the invitation and repeated that he would have to discuss it with Michelle.

'I hope you can persuade her,' Hannah replied, adding under her breath, 'I think I'm going to need something to keep me busy over the next couple of weeks.'

It would have been cruel to point out that blowing a load of money on an extravagant Christmas party was hardly going to help her business survive.

I was grateful to Hannah for including my family in her Christmas plans, and was really looking forward to seeing my mother and father, along with my sister and her husband and son. We all generally got on well together, and I was particularly fond of my nephew, Joel, whom Poppy adored. Sometimes my mother came to stay with me on her own, and the intensity of those visits veered crazily between genial and agonising. We had two main sources of disagreement. For no reason that I could fathom, my mother had convinced herself that I was unusually intelligent, even though my paltry achievements disproved that idea. She remained obdurate in her opinion that I was wasting my talents working in a menial job in an obscure village. She seemed to think I was working as a waitress to spite her, and nothing I said could dispel her delusion.

The other topic on which we couldn't agree was our divergent attitudes towards my single status. She had thankfully given up her efforts to persuade me that a woman could not possibly be happy unless she had a husband and children. With the prospect of an early marriage receding from me with every passing year, there was no boyfriend on the horizon, and I wasn't interested in having children. I was happy enough with Poppy and my circle of friends. Nevertheless, my mother was adamant that I must be lonely, insisting that Poppy was no substitute for a man. Of course she was right about that, but she was wrong in refusing to accept that I could possibly be content with only a dog for company.

In some ways, I was happier now than I had been when living with my former boyfriend. But although I would never admit it to my mother, I was sometimes lonely, despite my circle of good friends. Even my loyal companion, Poppy, couldn't fill the void my ex-boyfriend had left in my life when we had split up. Since then, I had been wary of entering into another relationship.

7

As a rule, Sunday was a relatively busy day at the tea shop. We started early, offering a choice of traditional breakfast dishes ranging from full English, complete with locally sourced sausages and eggs and fresh bread, to a cold vegan platter with avocado, humus, and salad. There was rarely a free table from nine o'clock when we opened, until two o'clock in the afternoon. We stopped serving breakfast at midday, at which point customers started coming in for lunch. For a couple of hours after that, we served countless filled baguettes and rolls, all freshly baked. From around two, we might have a relatively quiet patch for an hour or so, before afternoon tea customers arrived to pack the place out once again until we closed at six.

That Sunday, we had no customers at breakfast time. Neither of us mentioned the patisserie, although we couldn't help noticing a buzz of activity across the road when we arrived. I was in the kitchen laying out some scones, when Hannah came in. She looked upset.

I put down the plate I was holding. 'Hannah, what's wrong?'

'I went over the road,' she replied. 'You should see what's happening there.' She shook her head miserably, unable to carry on.

Troubled by her distress, I hurried through the empty café and out into the street. Moving past the Christmas tree gave me a clear view across the road, to where a huge gold sash hung across the patisserie with the words 'Grand Opening Today' emblazoned across it in large bold scarlet letters. All the lights on the front of the cake shop were flashing in a chaotic display of dazzling colours. A vulgar pavement sign advertised 'Everything Half Price'. In the absence of a trumpeter or a drum roll to attract attention, upbeat music spilled out onto the street. Had a circus parade turned up to disturb the quiet civility of the High Street, it could not have been more disruptive. In the line of people waiting for the doors of the patisserie to open, I recognised several of our regular customers.

By ten o'clock, the Sunshine Tea Shoppe was still empty, and the stream of people over the road was filing slowly into the patisserie. After another half an hour, Hannah announced she was closing and going home. I tried to persuade her to be patient, but she shook her head and said she wasn't going to hang around and watch her rival's triumphant opening.

'Don't give up,' I exclaimed fiercely. 'You can stay in the kitchen and bake and I'll wait here for customers.'

'What's the point when everyone's going over there? I'm not going to give her the satisfaction of seeing my humiliation,' she said with a stony expression.

'I'm sure there's nothing to worry about. The patisserie will be a flash in the pan, you'll see. You can't tell anything when they've only just opened. The years of hard graft you've put into this place count for more than a snazzy new window and a little local curiosity. She's untried and untested and I don't know why you think she'll succeed when everyone knows most new restaurants close almost as soon as they open. And in any case, a bit of healthy competition isn't necessarily a bad thing. It will help us keep on our toes.'

Hannah stared blankly at me before replying that she didn't need some jumped up French woman to keep her on her toes. With no customers in the tea shop, it was hard to argue with her when she insisted there was no point in staying open. Unable to think of anything to say that might cheer her up, I watched her leave in silence. Once she had gone, I collected Poppy from Jane's house. If she was surprised to see me so early, she didn't say so and neither of us mentioned Hannah or the tea shop.

'Poppy's been as good as gold,' Jane assured me, as she did every day.

Poppy ran over to Holly and nudged her. The old dog opened one eye and thumped her tail on the rug, before we left. Our way home led us down the High Street. Instead of trotting on towards the lane where we lived, Poppy slowed down as we drew near the tea shop.

'Hannah's not there,' I told her. 'Come on, we're going home.'

I gave her lead a tug, but she resisted. A large dog with an equally wilful temperament would have been difficult to handle, as she sometimes refused to go where I wanted. Poppy was small enough to be carried, so when she was being contrary, I usually just scooped her up in my arms and carried her wherever I wanted to go. When she persisted in trying to drag me towards the tea shop I was about to lean down and pick her up, when it occurred to me to take a peek through the window of the new patisserie and see who was in there. So I followed Poppy slowly to the Christmas tree, between the Sunshine Tea Shoppe and *Patisserie Desirée*. The queue to enter the patisserie was shorter now that the doors had opened. I saw a few of our regular customers through the window, and a few more waiting to go in. As I turned away, my attention was caught by a man standing in the doorway admitting people. He was wearing a navy suit and matching narrow tie over a pale blue shirt. I recognised the newcomer who had gone to Maud's shop to buy stacks of butter.

Without stopping to consider what I was doing, I joined the line, with Poppy standing quietly beside me. While we were shuffling slowly forwards, I studied the signs in the window. The patisserie had certainly made no attempt to blend in with the other shop fronts, each of which had a different colour scheme. The Sunshine Tea Shoppe was yellow, inside and out, Norman's awning was red and white as befitted a butcher's, and the hair and beauty salon was painted pink with touches of silver. They all looked attractive yet restrained. By contrast, the garish and fussy new unit jarred with the dignified character of the street. The name *Patisserie Desirée* was displayed in dazzling pink neon lights that shimmered against a bright red, blue and white background. An Eiffel Tower depicted in blue and red neon lights glowed on the left-hand side of the door, and a similarly brilliant image of a pink five tier cake plate and a pot of coffee shone from the window pane on the right of the door. The line of people inched forwards, past the dazzling display.

At last I reached the front of the queue, where the stranger rewarded my patience with a warm smile. Thanking me for waiting, he held the door open for me and ushered me to a small table in a corner by the Eiffel Tower window.

'I hope this is all right for you,' he murmured, leaning towards me and gazing into my eyes.

Poppy meanwhile had stayed close to my feet, and while he was talking she crept under the table. I wasn't sure the waiter had even noticed her, but decided against enquiring whether she could stay. I felt a pang of regret as he withdrew and hoped he would be back soon to take my order and give me an opportunity to engage him in conversation. After all, he had enquired about my relationship status. It was only polite to reciprocate. Before I could attempt to summon him back with a gesture, a glamorous woman manoeuvred her way towards me, her approach heralded by a powerful whiff of perfume. Her scarlet stiletto heels looked inappropriate for working in a café environment, her hair was piled on top of her head in layers that looked so stiff, they must have been doused in lacquer, and everything about her looked false: her hair, her nails, and her extravagant eyelashes. Yet beneath her heavy makeup I could see she had a lovely face, and her smile was warm and welcoming, as though she was genuinely pleased to see me.

She handed me an elaborately decorated menu, tapping the special offer with a long scarlet nail. I wondered how she managed in the kitchen, with nails like that. She greeted me, speaking with a pronounced French accent. Then she twirled around and sashayed away between the tables, hips swaying, leaving me with the menu. I studied it carefully, comparing it to what we offered at the tea shop. The dishes were listed in French, some of which I struggled to translate. Many of the words were recognisable: *croissants, baguettes, pain au chocolat, pain au raisins, brioche* and *éclair*. Others were unfamiliar. I had heard of a *croque monsieur* but was not sure what it was. As for *jambon-buerre* and *tarte aux mirabelles,* they were a mystery to me. All I could work out was that the first had something to do with butter, and the second was a tart of some description.

When the waiter came over to my table, I enquired about the unknown items and learned that '*jambon-buerre*' was nothing more exotic than a ham baguette, and *mirabelles* were a type of plum. Listening closely, I detected no hint of a French accent in his voice, which could have led me to ask him whether he came from France. However, the place was heaving and it seemed the wrong moment to try and question him about his life. After a moment's indecision, I asked him if there was anything he could recommend. He began giving me details of the various cakes and pastries and I decided on a slice of plum pie, with cream. He told me that was an excellent choice, and one of his favourites, and I felt a glow of satisfaction at his approbation. With a nod, he noted down my order before enquiring what I would like to drink. I ordered coffee, as tea didn't seem appropriate in a French café.

Gazing around after he had gone, I saw that just about everyone there was a regular at Hannah's tea shop. It was painful to acknowledge that our regular customers were indeed fickle, but that seemed to be the case. Feeling uncomfortable, I stared at my table and hoped the waiter would return soon with my order so that I could gulp it down and leave. I half hoped the service would be poor, but I didn't have to wait long and he brought my pie and coffee at the same time. It just remained for the pastries to be delicious, and Hannah's rout would be complete. The waiter smiled so cordially when he brought my tray, I wondered again if he was flirting with me. Aware that the impression was probably just wishful thinking on my part, I smiled back. It was tempting to ask him whether the pie was as tasty as he was, but of course I couldn't make such an embarrassing confession of my feelings when we hadn't even really met. If I had been a lascivious old man, and he a pretty young girl, I would have been had for sexual harassment.

He leaned across to put my pie down in front of me. With mixed feelings, I realised it was obvious from the aroma that the pastry was freshly baked. As the waiter was putting my coffee on the table, I heard a sound of scuffling from under my chair and Poppy peeped out, growling. Before I could tell her to be quiet, she sprang out, barking at the waiter. Startled, he jumped back and dropped the coffee. The pot smashed on the floor tiles with a resounding crash. I lunged forward and grabbed Poppy before she could reach the shards of china and spilt coffee. Everyone turned to look. Several people glared at me, muttering. Someone laughed.

'What is this animal doing here?' a heavily accented female voice demanded.

I bridled at the woman's tone, and the way she said 'animal', while Poppy continued snarling and growling.

'Get that animal out of here,' the French woman snapped angrily. 'This is a patisserie, where people come to eat. We do not permit dogs.'

'Very well,' I retorted, equally furious, and jumping to my feet. 'We know where we're not wanted, don't we, Poppy? As for your menu,' I went on, controlling my temper with difficulty and lying frostily, 'I find it very disappointing. I don't suppose you even do your own baking here. The tea shop over the road serves homemade cakes and scones, fresh from the oven every day.'

'I hope they do not allow dogs there.' She wrinkled her perfectly shaped nose, as though to intimate that dogs were unhygienic.

'It is only a small dog,' the waiter said in a conciliatory tone.

Poppy growled at him but I felt a rush of gratitude for his understanding. Without another word, I grabbed my coat. As I yanked it off the back of my chair, it swung round and swept everything off the table in front of me. Pie and cream flew through the air to land at the French woman's feet, splashing her red shoes with crumbs of pastry mixed with flecks of white. Poppy wriggled frantically in my arms, desperate to jump down so she could reach the spilt cream, which she loved. The owner shrieked and I clung on tightly to Poppy, afraid she might cut herself on the broken china. The handsome waiter threw me an apologetic glance. I wanted to ask him if he planned on going to the village pub that evening, but it was hardly the moment to invite him to join me later for a drink. I would have to find another way to make contact with him. Clearly, we wouldn't be seeing one another again in the *Patisserie Desirée*.

8

On Monday morning, I was up early, optimistic that our regular customers at the Sunshine Tea Shoppe would be back. After dropping Poppy off at Jane's house, my relief on returning to my normal routine working with my best friend was short-lived; the tea shop remained empty when we opened the door. We waited, but the usual breakfast rush never materialised. Approaching December, it was soon obvious that Hannah's profit for the period would be significantly lower than in previous years. We sat down together with a pot of tea and I commiserated with her, wretchedly aware that my job could be under threat. If the tea shop lost too much money, Hannah might have to go back to relying on Jane to help out during busy periods as she had done before my arrival in Ashton Mead. Worse, the tea shop might have to close altogether.

Hannah was convinced our competitor over the road was responsible for our reduced takings. Even though she was probably right, I did my best to reassure her that everything was going to be fine.

'The patisserie's only just opened. People are bound to be curious,' I said. 'It's only natural, but I'm sure that's all it is.'

Hannah wasn't the only one who was panicking. I was nervous whenever she mentioned the competition. Had I been confident no one else would mention it, I wouldn't have told her about my visit to the patisserie. Knowing how rapidly news spread around the village, I wondered whether it would be best to admit to having checked out our competition, before she could hear about it from anyone else. By mid-morning, we still had no breakfast trade. Hannah continued to rant about the patisserie poaching our customers until eventually I could bear my guilty secret no longer and confessed. For a moment Hannah stared at me in silence when I finished speaking. Then she stood up, walked over to the entrance, turned the sign around and locked the door. She remained motionless for a few seconds, standing with her back to me, while I waited anxiously for her response. Finally she spun round and stared mournfully at me.

'What were you thinking?' she demanded. 'Even my own best friend goes there – at least I thought you were my friend.' And with that, she burst into tears.

Clearly it wasn't only my actions that had upset her, but my visit to the patisserie must have been the last straw for her, and I felt terrible.

'Sit down, please,' I urged her. 'You have to let me explain.'

'Go on then. Explain,' she sniffed vigorously. 'I really want to know why you went there behind my back.'

'It wasn't behind your back,' I protested.

There was a great deal more I could have said about being at liberty to go wherever I liked, whenever I liked. The fact that she paid my wages didn't give her the right to control my movements, and my decisions were my own. But on balance I decided to keep my indignation to myself, at least while she was so upset. The last thing I wanted to do was fall out with her when she was in trouble.

'Well, you didn't bother to run the idea past me first,' she said crossly.

'I didn't discuss it with you because I had no intention of going anywhere near the patisserie,' I said. 'There was nothing premeditated about it. But then Poppy dragged me along the High Street. I think she wanted to come here, but you had closed up and gone home. And all right, I admit it, I was curious to see what it was like in there, just the once. I thought it might be a good idea to take a look, size the place up, see what they were offering,' I concluded lamely.

'Well, go on then, don't stop there. What was it like?' she asked, wiping her eyes on a serviette as she sat down. 'I want to hear all about it. Every single detail. And don't spare my feelings. I might as well know the worst. How amazing was it?'

'I'll make us a fresh pot of tea and tell you everything,' I replied. 'Although, to be honest, there's not much to tell, because they threw us out. It was a bit of a disaster, really. I've never been thrown out of a café before. At least I got a pot of coffee out of her, even if it did end up all over the floor.'

I grinned apologetically, and Hannah giggled, although she appeared to be crying at the same time. I hurried off to the kitchen to make the tea which I brought out with two fat fruit scones. If no one else was coming to the tea shop, I figured we might as well not let the fresh scones go to waste. Our view of the patisserie was partly obscured by the enormous Christmas tree standing in the middle of the street. All the same, by tacit agreement we sat facing away from the street, and I poured the tea.

'There's no point in throwing these scones away,' I said, smothering mine in a thick layer of butter.

'We could have frozen them,' she replied, spreading lashings of jam and cream on hers. 'You know we can't afford to waste anything.'

I ignored her rejoinder; under the circumstances I thought we both deserved a scone, if not two or three. As we ate, I did my best to describe the French woman. To begin with, she had seemed quite pleasant, but I kept that impression to myself. Once she had objected to Poppy, any sympathy I had felt for her immediately vanished. That made it easy for me to refrain from saying anything positive about her, which might only have upset Hannah all over again. I was keen to make my friend feel supported, not betrayed, by my disastrous visit to the patisserie. When it came to the part where Poppy had startled the waiter into dropping my coffee, Hannah gave a reluctant smile. At the account of my coat accidentally sending my plum pie and cream flying after the coffee, she laughed out loud and said she wished she had been there to see it.

'I suppose a lot of people saw what happened,' she added seriously. 'Do you think everyone will suspect you did it on purpose? They might think I put you up to it.'

I hadn't thought of that, and the idea made me uneasy. But no one could accuse Hannah of having asked Poppy to startle the waiter. Just then, a group of people appeared outside. Dabbing at her eyes, Hannah hurried to open the door and assure them we were open. It was business as usual as we welcomed a dozen Japanese tourists who wanted to sample a traditional English tea. By the time they left, Hannah had cheered up and we remained open for the rest of the afternoon, serving a trickle of customers until it was time to close the door for the day and fetch Poppy from Jane's house. Poppy jumped up and ran to me, growling with pleasure at seeing me again.

As usual, Jane asked me how my day had gone, and I gave her a summary of my visit to the patisserie. She laughed when I reached the part where my coffee had spilt all over the floor.

'Was it hot?' she gasped, still laughing. 'Oh dear, I shouldn't laugh. Poppy could have been hurt!'

Hearing her name, Poppy wagged her tail, and Jane leaned down to pet her.

Assuring Jane that I had grabbed Poppy and hoisted her onto my lap before she could reach the broken pot and spilt coffee, I proceeded to give an account of my coat sweeping the whole plate of pie and cream off the table. Much to Poppy's frustration, I had refused to put her down.

'So you didn't get to try out the French baking, after all?' Jane nodded, grinning. 'Well, that sounds like a complete waste of time. I hope you didn't pay for the coffee? I mean,' she went on, 'it was her fault for letting Poppy in and then wanting to chuck her out. That's no way to run a business. She let you in under false pretences.'

Remembering how the waiter had been looking at me when he failed to notice Poppy at the entrance to the patisserie, I began to remonstrate, but Jane was determined to censure anything Hannah's competitor was doing. She insisted that once a customer had been admitted with a dog, they shouldn't be thrown out on the grounds that they had brought a dog with them. I couldn't argue with her.

That evening, I met my group of friends in the pub. To my relief, Hannah seemed to be back to her usual self, and appeared to have forgiven me for going to the patisserie. Adam had mentioned it to his father, Richard, and both they and Toby wanted to hear all about Hannah's competition. None of them had been there, no doubt out of loyalty to Hannah, and I felt embarrassed that they all knew about my visit.

'I suppose Hannah sent you there to spy out the competition?' Richard asked me in a theatrical whisper, a broad grin creasing his round cheeks. 'Industrial espionage comes to Ashton Mead!' he added dramatically, with a wink.

Even Hannah giggled, and I felt slightly less awkward, which I suspected had been Richard's intention. As the sole residents of Mill Lane, which boasted only two properties, we had struck up a friendship which had been cemented by Poppy's attachment to him. By the time I had recounted my catastrophic visit to the patisserie, we were all laughing at Poppy's exploits and my own clumsiness. Having completed my catalogue of disasters, I looked up and saw the waiter from the patisserie watching me from the bar.

'He didn't hear what I was saying, did he?' I muttered to Hannah.

'Who?'

Pointing out the waiter, I decided not to mention where he worked, instead telling Hannah how we had met in Maud's shop.

'And why are you interested in him, I wonder?' she replied, studying him for a moment before giving me a knowing smile.

'No reason,' I said, with an exaggeratedly innocent expression.

She giggled, and I knew she had forgiven me for going to the patisserie without first discussing the idea with her. I was considering going up to the bar, where I might by chance happen to stand next to the waiter and strike up a conversation, but before I could clamber to my feet, Barry joined us. He pulled up a chair and parked himself next to me, calling out to Cliff to bring over another round of drinks as he lowered himself onto his seat, inadvertently blocking my view of the waiter.

'My aunt would like to thank you in person,' he told me. 'She's very grateful to you for keeping things going at the shop. You did a great job. Any time you're free, she's hoping you'll pop in to see her.' He smiled at me. 'We both really appreciate what you did. I'm very fond of my aunt, you know.'

'It was you, not me, who held everything together while she was away,' I protested. 'If it hadn't been for you, I wouldn't have had a clue what to do. Half the time, I couldn't even get the blinking card reader to work, and as for keeping track of the stock and what we needed to reorder, I honestly had no idea what we needed. It would have been utter carnage if it had all been left to me.'

Barry grinned and looked embarrassed at being

thanked. He shifted in his seat and, looking up, I saw that the waiter from the patisserie had left his post at the bar. Shrugging off my regret, I had to accept that once again I had missed my chance to speak to him. When the next opportunity presented itself, I vowed to be ready.

SINCE WE HAD ALMOST fallen out, throughout the following week Hannah and I were careful to avoid even a hint of discord between us. We both valued our friendship, and I suspected the prospect of friction between us bothered her as much as it did me. I had been looking forward to returning to the tea shop, but my anticipation had been tainted by the thought of the rival establishment over the road. Every time we went in or out of the tea shop, and every time we walked along the High Street to the pub, it was impossible to avoid seeing the dazzling lights of *Patisserie Desirée*. Sharing my friend's fears for the future, I knew her too well to be taken in by her jaunty air. When I went in the kitchen, more often than not, I caught her muttering darkly about the French woman who was threatening to close the Sunshine Tea Shoppe.

Admittedly I hadn't invested all my money in the tea shop; I had very little money to invest anywhere. If Hannah's business failed, I stood to lose nothing but my job, which could be replaced. Waitressing posts tended to be ephemeral and there were plenty of cafés and restaurants in the nearby town of Swindon. But I would never find another position where the boss was my friend, I was able to walk to work, and Poppy could accompany me whenever Jane wasn't available to look after her. For three years, my life had revolved around Hannah and her tea shop, and I had never been happier. In every way, other than romantically, she had become the most significant person in my life. So leaving aside my own selfish considerations, it hurt me to see Hannah so troubled.

Meanwhile, it was difficult to forget about the patisserie which was looming so large in our lives. Not only in the pub and Maud's shop, but even in the Sunshine Tea Shoppe I overheard customers discussing it. One woman in the grocery shop was tactless enough to ask me for my opinion of the new French café, when I was in there doing some shopping one day. When I answered, somewhat disingenuously, that I hadn't been able to try it yet, the woman sniffed and stared at me with a sceptical expression, while her companion pulled her aside and whispered furiously in her ear. She must have been sharing the gossip about my humiliating experience at the patisserie. I pretended to ignore them; it was hard to believe people could be so insensitive.

Back in the empty tea shop, the bell jangled, and I was thrilled to see the good-looking waiter from the patisserie enter. My face felt suddenly hot, and I was afraid he would notice me blushing. Forcing myself to breathe deeply in a conscious effort to remain calm, I smiled in welcome as he approached me.

'Mademoiselle,' he said, with a curious little bow that

was absurd yet endearing at the same time. 'Allow me to introduce myself. My name is Niles.'

Flashing a smile, he leaned towards me and asked me softly whether he could borrow some sugar. On his lips, the question sounded intimate. Returning his smile, I told him my name, wondering if I dared flirt shamelessly with him. I was trying to decide what to say to him when Hannah emerged from the kitchen.

'Hello,' Hannah greeted him, seeing me grinning foolishly and looking flustered. 'I don't think we've met?' I felt myself blush again, and hoped he hadn't noticed her wink at me.

'Hello,' Niles replied, holding out his hand. 'I'm Niles.'

'Are you stopping long in the village?' she enquired politely, as he bent to kiss her hand with exaggerated formality.

'I live close by,' he told her. 'I moved here recently from France.'

'Welcome to Ashton Mead,' she said. 'I'm Hannah. I own this tea shop. I think you've met Emily?' She gestured towards me. 'She works here with me. You might want to try our excellent homemade cakes and scones. We make them fresh every day, and they're very popular.'

She didn't explain that sometimes she put them in the freezer as soon as they cooled down, and heated them up again before serving them. She was adamant that was the same as serving them when they came straight out of the oven for the first time. To be fair, it was impossible to tell the difference between the fresh and the freshly frozen once they came out of the oven.

Niles inclined his head. 'I have heard about your tea rooms,' he said. 'And your reputation as a baker is legendary in the village.'

Hannah grinned, murmuring modestly that he was flattering her. 'Please, take a seat,' she said.

'Alas, I cannot stay,' he replied. 'My own cake shop is just across the street from here, and I must return to work without delay. You will have seen us? We opened very recently.'

Hannah took a step backwards, narrowly missing barging into a table. 'Do you mean to tell me you own the new French patisserie?' she demanded in a strangled voice, wide-eyed with surprise.

'Own it? Sadly, no,' he replied, turning his head to smile at me. 'But I work there, as Emily can attest.'

'Niles was asking if he could borrow some sugar,' I stammered.

Hannah crossed her arms and glared at him. 'First you poach my customers,' she hissed, 'and now...' she frowned. 'Now you think you can come in here and help yourself to my sugar.'

I swore under my breath, but Hannah was too wound up to notice my disquiet. Her cheeks turned pink and she stepped forwards, raising her voice. 'You can tell your boss, if she keeps on like this, she'll regret it. She's making a big mistake if she thinks she can muscle her way in and take my place in the village. Her patisserie is never going to eclipse my tea shop. Tell her if she doesn't leave, I'm going to make her sorry she ever came to Ashton Mead. No one wants her here. Next time she crosses me, she'll get what's coming to her, if I have to slash my prices to rock bottom. Tell her I'll do whatever it takes to get rid of her and her fancy French pastries.' With a theatrical flourish, she stepped back, accidentally knocking over a chair which fell to the floor with a loud clatter.

Only then did I notice that two women had come in. They were local residents who often came to the café for tea and cakes. Hearing Hannah's raised voice, they hovered on the threshold before turning and scurrying away without saying a word. As they left, I noticed both of them were clutching their phones. They might have taken them out for any number of reasons, but it seemed likely they had been gleefully recording videos of Hannah's outburst. In any case, from the looks on their faces, they had evidently heard enough of her rant to draw their own conclusions about what was going on. No doubt they were off to tell everyone they met that Hannah was threatening to destroy the new patisserie, together with its owner. In a small village like Ashton Mead, where rumours tended to become exaggerated with each retelling, I trembled to think what stories might soon be circulating about Hannah behind her back.

Throughout it all, Niles maintained a dignified silence, seemingly unperturbed by Hannah's fury. Once he had left, I turned to her, and saw that she was physically shaking.

'I can't believe I spoke to him like that,' she blurted out, and burst into tears, mumbling that she wasn't an aggressive person.

Hurriedly locking the door, I reassured her that it was only words, spoken in the heat of the moment, and there was no harm done. Niles probably hadn't even heard what she had said.

'He might remember you were miffed about something, but I don't think he was paying much attention. I had the impression you were talking too quickly for him to follow. To be honest, I really don't think he was listening. You know what men are like. As far as he was concerned, you could have been having a go at me for something,' I concluded awkwardly.

Hannah nodded uncertainly. I didn't tell her that, behind her back, two village gossips had witnessed her diatribe and, unlike Niles, they had been paying close attention and would no doubt recall every word she had flung at him. It was even possible they had recorded it on their phones, and were already broadcasting her rant to an audience greedy for tittle-tattle. I put my arms around her and stroked her tousled blonde curls, murmuring that everything was going to be all right, but my reassurances must have sounded as hollow to her as they felt to me. Before long, everyone in the village would have heard how she had threatened the proprietor of the French patisserie. I wondered how many people would feel sympathy for her when they heard about her outburst, which would no doubt be grossly exaggerated with each iteration.

10

As November wore on, the temperature remained mild. There were reports of widespread floods in the South of England and deep snow in the North of Scotland. Although we escaped any extreme weather conditions in our little village, we had our fair share of rain and the river ran higher and faster than usual. It was dry as Poppy and I set out on our way to the pub that Friday evening, but the sky was overcast and it began to drizzle as we neared our destination. I avoided squelching on the waterlogged grassy verges, so as not to dirty my boots, but Poppy rambled everywhere. Heedless of mud and puddles, she sniffed around busily while I urged her along as quickly as possible, afraid of being caught in a heavy downpour. Entering the bar, I looked around while wiping my boots, which were dirty in spite of my efforts to avoid walking where it was muddy. Barry and Toby were already there, seated at a table and deep in conversation. Adam arrived soon after me and we sat down with our two friends. After greeting us, Toby headed over to the bar to chat with Michelle.

'Where's Hannah?' I asked.

'She'll be along soon,' Adam replied. 'She stayed at home to take some more cakes out of the oven.' He shrugged. 'She's going bonkers filling the freezer. We'd better all starve ourselves for the next few weeks, because she'll be offended if we don't stuff our faces over Christmas.' He grinned.

After a moment, Adam followed Toby to the bar, leaving me and Barry sitting together. As Barry was offering to buy me a drink, Hannah arrived, shaking drops of rain from her hair and brushing them from the shoulders of her coat before she took it off. Adam called out to her, gesturing that he was buying her a drink, and she nodded and smiled at him.

'Is it raining much?' Barry asked her, as she sat down.

'Just drizzling, but it's more like sleet. I think it might snow overnight,' she replied with a mock shiver.

'Not according to the forecast,' Adam said, coming over and sitting down. 'I heard it's going to stay wet but it won't freeze over Christmas.'

It might have been my imagination, but I thought a few of the locals threw inquisitive glances at Hannah. A small group of people appeared to be muttering ominously, their eyes alighting briefly on her before flicking away again. I did my best to keep talking, determined to distract her from the attention she was attracting. She seemed unaware of their curiosity, and chatted happily about her plans for Christmas.

Cliff was collecting empty glasses and overheard our conversation. 'I read that they're predicting a White Christmas,' he said. 'The forecasts are pretty accurate these days.'

'Oh, I hope it snows for Christmas,' Hannah replied, clapping her hands.

Cliff grunted. 'As long as it doesn't stop my customers getting here. I heard there may be blizzards on their way.'

'In Ashton Mead?' Hannah protested. 'I doubt it.'

'Have you been following the forecasts?' Cliff asked her and she shook her head.

'There you are then,' he replied, as though that confirmed what he had said.

We all agreed that we would come to the party in the pub. After yet another discussion about the party for the village children, Hannah asked Toby whether he and Michelle had decided where they were planning to spend Christmas Day. She beamed when he told her they would like to stay in Ashton Mead and spend the day with all of us, and his mother, before going to see Michelle's parents on Boxing Day.

'If we're still invited to lunch at the tea shop, that is,' he added.

'Of course you are,' she grinned. 'You know you're always welcome.'

'It'll be just me and Michelle, and mum, of course.'

About to reply, Hannah frowned, and I turned my head to see Niles standing at the bar. His cheeks were ruddy from the cold, and his eyes looked lively and bright as he nodded and smiled at me. He seemed on the point of coming over to join us but, as he was walking towards us, Hannah scowled and shook her head at him and he stopped abruptly.

'There's no need to be unfriendly to him,' Adam said, seeing her expression. Hannah must have told him about her day, because he added, 'It's hardly his fault if Desirée sent him over to borrow some sugar. He works there.'

'Yes,' I agreed eagerly. 'You can't blame Niles for what happened. He just works there. How would he know how you feel about the patisserie opening up over the road?'

Hannah looked at me and gave an apologetic shrug. 'I suppose you think I'm being unreasonable,' she muttered. 'Go on then, ask him to join us if you want to.'

Toby was listening to the conversation with a slightly puzzled expression. 'What are you all talking about?' he asked. 'What have I missed?'

Hannah pointed Niles out and explained that he worked at the new patisserie. 'Emily fancies him,' she added.

I was cross with her for blabbing about my secret crush, but Toby merely shrugged, while Adam didn't appear to have heard what she said. Looking crestfallen, Barry blurted out that he had just remembered something he needed to do, and he rose to his feet and left.

'Poor Barry,' Hannah murmured, watching him go.

'Why?' I asked, feeling defensive, even though I had done nothing wrong.

'You must know how he feels about you,' Hannah replied.

'Yes, and he knows how I feel about him. It's not my fault if he's keen on me, and I really wish he wasn't.'

'He can't help how he feels,' Hannah said.

'Well, neither can I. It's not as if I've ever done anything to encourage him.'

Hannah fell silent, perhaps thinking that I had once gone on an unsuccessful date with Barry. Toby began talking about a local junior football league which his school had won, while I watched Niles surreptitiously. When he turned round, I managed to catch his eye and smile at him. We gazed at one another for a few seconds and I felt a thrill of nervous anticipation. It was a long time since I had been in a serious relationship with a man. There were very few attractive men of around my age living in the village. So, as far as I was concerned, Niles was an extremely interesting addition to our community.

The next time Niles looked in my direction, I gave a little wave and smiled at him. Taking the hint, he made his way towards us, carrying his pint carefully. Noticing his hand was shaking, I was thrilled to see that he looked as jittery as I was feeling. There was space for Niles to pull a chair over and sit next to me. As he leaned forward to set his pint down on the table, Poppy dashed out from under the table, yapping furiously. She had a surprisingly loud bark for such a small dog, and several people turned to glare at her. Startled, Niles knocked over his pint. Luckily the glass didn't shatter but rolled across the table, spilling beer everywhere, splashing Adam and Toby, and drenching me. I gasped as the cold liquid soaked through my jeans to my legs. Poppy, the cause of the mishap, ran forward to lick up the spilled drink. Quickly I reached down to grab her and lift her onto my lap, away from the pool of beer. Disappointed, she fussed and groused for a few moments, but I held her firmly and she resigned herself to licking my beer-soaked jeans. Mortified, Niles let out an involuntary curse before apologising to everyone for the accident.

'That dog is a menace,' I overheard someone at a nearby table say.

'Shouldn't be allowed in here,' another voice chimed in.

'Poppy doesn't seem to share your liking for Niles,' Hannah murmured to me with a wry smile. 'Perhaps you should follow her instincts. She usually seems to be right about people.'

Michelle bustled over, armed with a bucket of cleaning materials, and started mopping the floor. Niles gallantly offered to do it for her, but she shook her head, insisting it wouldn't take a moment to clean up.

'It happens all the time,' she said, which wasn't true. In the three years that I had been going to the pub, I had never before seen someone tip over a whole pint of beer, although Barry had once managed to spill a plate of fish and chips on our one date. The memory of it still made me cringe.

We moved our chairs to give Michelle room for her mopping, while Niles insisted on wiping the table, apologising profusely for his clumsiness. Cliff brought over a fresh pint for Niles and refused to let him pay for it.

'We look after our customers here,' he assured Niles. 'Especially the new ones,' he added, winking at the rest of us. 'So don't you lot go getting any ideas.'

I was watching the way Niles's straw-coloured hair flopped forward over his brow, and thinking how fit he was, when he turned and caught me staring at him.

'Your dog may be cute, but he seems hostile,' he said, with more than a touch of asperity. 'I don't think he likes me very much.'

'Poppy's female,' I corrected him, holding her firmly on my lap. 'And she's actually very friendly.'

Poppy bristled and gave a warning growl as though to contradict me.

'She thinks she's protecting me,' I added, feeling embarrassed by her aggression. 'She's wary of strangers, that's all. She'll be fine once she gets to know you.'

That wasn't strictly true either. Somehow Niles seemed to possess a knack of causing other people to fib, although I was only telling a white lie because he was a newcomer to the village and I was keen for him to feel comfortable with us. Although Poppy often barked at other dogs, she was rarely hostile towards people, even strangers. It was true that she had occasionally taken against people before. They had always turned out to be threatening my happiness in some way, which only proved she was protective towards me. Once she accepted Niles into our lives, I was sure she would be fine. Toby and Adam assured Niles that there was no harm done, and I echoed their reassurances gratefully, despite having received a lapful of cold beer. Hannah joined us in telling Niles that no one blamed him for what had obviously been an accident. He sat down next to me but when he leaned towards me, Poppy warned him off with a low growl that rumbled in her throat.

It was my turn to issue a warning. 'No barking, Poppy,' I commanded her, and she turned her head to look at me with a baleful expression. 'There's no point in looking at me like that,' I added, trying to sound stern. 'We all saw what you did. That's the second time you've startled Niles and made him spill something. First it was my coffee, and now his beer. Don't do it again.' I turned to Niles. 'I think she understands.'

Poppy looked quizzically at me, then let out a single bark and wagged her tail as if to say she understood better than I realised. She didn't appear abashed by my reprimand. Doing my best to ignore my wet legs, I joined in the conversation around the table, which centred on Niles and what he could reveal about the new patisserie. He told us that he hadn't worked for Desirée before the patisserie opened in Ashton Mead, adding that she seemed to be a reasonable employer. He explained that she was French, but since he was bilingual, that presented no problem. On the contrary, he said, it made him indispensable to her as her English was limited. I wanted to ask him if he had worked in France, but didn't want to interrupt his account. Instead I listened avidly, looking forward to telling my mother that my new boyfriend spoke fluent French. Not that he was my boyfriend, yet, but from the way he singled me out and kept smiling at me, I was hopeful that he soon would be.

After a while, Hannah and Adam went home, and Toby wandered over to chat to Michelle, leaving me and Niles alone together. Poppy was restless, and gave a menacing growl every time Niles spoke to me. I managed to subdue her, but it was difficult to listen to him while she was squirming on my lap and snapping whenever he opened his mouth. He carried on without allowing her antics to distract him. If anything, he was more attentive to me than ever. Gazing into my eyes, he paid me compliments which, coming from anyone else, might have seemed extravagant, yet somehow on his lips sounded sincere. He told me that he had never been so fascinated by a woman before, and he found me irresistible. Listening to his flattery, I felt ten feet tall and devastatingly beautiful, and it wasn't just the alcohol that was making me feel exhilarated. Finally I had met a man who appreciated me. Not only that, but he was gorgeous. I could have sat watching him all night, basking in his attention, and was disappointed when he heaved himself to his feet.

'It's time I headed off,' he said. 'Goodnight, Emily.' Hearing my name on his lips felt like a caress. 'Before I leave, can I take your phone number?'

Hastily I scribbled my number on a beer mat and handed it to him. I wanted to beg him to stay, but was afraid of appearing needy. Instead, I stood up, hoping he would offer to walk me home, but he turned away and strode off. After the door closed behind him, I realised he hadn't given me his phone number and I didn't know where he lived. I consoled myself with the knowledge that the village was a small and intimate environment; even if he didn't call me, we were certain to see each other again soon. As soon as Niles had gone, Poppy jumped down, wagging her tail happily. We said goodnight to Toby, who was waiting for Michelle's shift to finish, and prepared to go out into the freezing cold night. Once Niles had gone, there was no reason for me to stay. I peered through the window, hoping to catch a glimpse of him as he passed a street light, but he had vanished into the darkness.

11

OLD BERT WAS HUNCHED over a table in his habitual corner near the door. He seemed to have taken up residence there, because he was sitting there whenever I went to the pub, and I never caught sight of him anywhere else in the village. He sat, nursing the dregs of a pint, and watching people as they went up to the bar. Although Cliff never glanced over in the corner, he must have been aware of the old man, because every once in a while he would jerk his head in Bert's direction. If the customer nodded, Cliff would take a pint over to the corner. Once I bought the old man several packets of nuts and crisps. He glared at me as though I was trying to poison him, as his jaws worked. For a moment, I was afraid he was going to spit on the floor. After that I conformed to the unspoken rule, and occasionally paid for a pint for him and nothing else. Cliff seemed to remember who had bought his drinks, and managed to spread the cost out fairly among the regulars. We were never asked to pay for Bert's beer more than once every few months, even though he was there every day. I thought that was an impressive feat of memory on Cliff's part, until Michelle confided that he kept a list behind the bar and ticked us off when it was our turn. Even so, Cliff gave Bert more pints than were paid for.

'Who is Bert?' I asked Maud one day, wondering if he was a relative of Cliff's who had fallen on hard times. But even Maud had no idea where he had come from.

'He just turned up in the pub one evening,' she told me. 'And he never left.'

'He must go home when the pub shuts,' I replied. 'He must live somewhere.'

She shrugged her narrow shoulders. 'That he must,' she agreed.

Serving a few last orders, Cliff took a pint over to Bert, while Michelle busied herself gathering up glasses and wiping tables and Toby sat waiting for her to finish. Zipping up my coat, I left the warmth of the pub for the cold night. The silence was a relief. In the pub it was sometimes an effort to hear what other people were saying against a constant background hubbub of conversation, and I had been on edge, trying to listen to Niles and offer appropriate responses to his compliments while keeping Poppy under control.

We walked swiftly away from the bright lights and clamorous interior of The Plough, where a few customers were still sitting around chatting and drinking. I usually found the night air invigorating when I took Poppy outside at the end of the day. On this occasion it was too cold to enjoy being outside, probably because my jeans were still damp.

Now that Poppy and I were alone, I was able to think about Niles without interruption. Recalling our conversation, it irked me that he hadn't offered to walk me home. Either Poppy had spooked him, or else he had been nervous of being rejected. Mentally running through everything he had said to me, I realised that although he had been very complimentary towards me, he hadn't invited me out or suggested we spend time together. Barry had been more forthcoming in his pursuit of me, even after I had made it clear that he wasn't getting anywhere with me. It seemed unlikely that Poppy would have completely put Niles off, if he was genuinely interested in me. I had to conclude that he had held back from asking me out because my reaction to his flattering comments had appeared lukewarm, if not downright dismissive. The truth was that, overwhelmed by his attention, I had probably come across as uninterested. The next time we met, I resolved to be less inhibited in my responses.

Preoccupied with thinking about Niles, I scarcely noticed how far we had walked until we were nearly at the tea shop. The tall Christmas tree loomed up ahead, shimmering brightly against the dark sky. Poppy, who had been trotting along quite happily, abruptly stopped in her tracks and began to whimper. I urged her to hurry, and tried to pull her along, but she refused to go any further. It wasn't raining but the air was damp, and I suspected she was hoping to go into the tea shop to warm up and enjoy some late night scraps, even though we very rarely went there at night. It was too cold to stand around, waiting for her to decide to walk on, so I picked her up. Holding her close to my chest, I could feel her trembling, and she continued to whimper. It was unusual for her to be agitated when she was outdoors, with so many scents to sniff, and I was worried in case she was sick. Murmuring gentle reassurances that we would soon be home and warm, I hurried on.

As we drew level with the tea shop, she let out a warning bark. I looked around, expecting to see a fox sauntering along the High Street. We occasionally saw them on the roads, especially at night, but the street was still and silent. It was too cold to dawdle so I started to walk quickly, but Poppy grew increasingly restless and finally she jumped down onto the pavement and began tugging at her lead, trying to drag me across the road. Not until then did it occur to me that Niles might be at the patisserie, working on his preparations for the morning. Perhaps Poppy was trying to make up for her earlier belligerence towards him by taking me to see him. It seemed unlikely, but once I had entertained the possibility, I couldn't resist going to have a look.

There were no lights on inside the patisserie, as far as I could see, but Poppy kept pulling me towards it, and I followed her, hoping to see Niles. Staring into the darkness through the patisserie window, I stumbled and nearly tripped over. Looking down, in the golden glow of Christmas tree lights I made out a dark shape on the pavement. It looked like a bundle of garbage and I wondered fleetingly if Desirée had left her rubbish out, thereby attracting a fox. But even as the thought flashed through my mind, I knew that we hadn't seen any foxes that night. In the same instant, I caught sight of a pair of elegant white legs sticking out of the bundle, which I now realised was a woman's body. A bright red stiletto-heeled shoe hung off one of the feet, and I saw its partner abandoned nearby on the wet pavement.

For a long moment, I stood transfixed. Then Poppy barked, recalling me to the situation. Hardly daring to breathe, I stole forwards. Whether the woman lying there was drunk or unconscious, she was likely to die of hypothermia unless she was moved soon. Tentatively I murmured her name, 'Desirée!' but she didn't respond. I called to her more loudly and drew closer. Reaching out, I took hold of her arm and shook her, shouting to her to wake up. Her eyelids didn't even flicker. She was lying with her feet towards the lights of the Christmas tree, and her face was hidden in shadow. Her elaborate hairstyle had come undone, and a few strands of long blonde hair lay spread out on the pavement around her like pallid seaweed. My fingers fumbled as I fished my phone out of my bag. I had to remove my gloves to touch the screen, and by the time I managed to switch on my phone torch, my fingers were aching with cold. The narrow beam of light wobbled around erratically, as I directed it along the length of the motionless body forming a shapeless mass at my feet.

At the sight of a ghastly face, pale as the frosty pavement on which it lay, I started back in alarm. It looked barely human, a macabre mask from a horror film. Thick black smudges bordered sightless eyes which seemed to gaze up at the sky in astonishment. With a shudder I understood that those staring eyes would never see again. Her black eyeliner had smeared, forming ugly streaks down both cheeks, and a rictus of terror stretched her bright red lips across her face like a gash. My fingers were nearly frozen but I managed to hit the emergency key on my phone and summon an ambulance, even though Desirée was clearly past help. I wondered whether to try and cover her face, or at least close her eyes, but was reluctant to touch her. It would make no difference to her now, and the ambulance would be arriving soon, before any scavengers could find her. I shivered and scrambled backwards, out of reach of the body.

There was nothing more to do, so I hurried across the road to shelter in the Sunshine Tea Shoppe, holding Poppy in my arms to share our body heat. She felt like a little hot water bottle in my arms. Having lit the oven to warm us up, I filled Poppy's water bowl and broke up a sausage roll for her before putting the kettle on and settling down to wait. Poppy seemed reinvigorated now we were no longer in the presence of the dead body, and appeared to be enjoying her night time adventure. Having demolished her sausage roll, she looked at me and wagged her tail, as if to say, 'I told you we should come in here out of the cold'.

As my tea was brewing, I heard the muffled purr of an engine. Leaving the kitchen for the front room of the tea shop, I watched an ambulance draw up behind the Christmas tree. At the same time, my phone rang. With a sigh, I turned the oven off and locked up and we left the warmth of the tea shop. Poppy whimpered as she followed me outside, into the freezing cold and damp of the night. We walked around to the other side of the ambulance, and saw a paramedic squatting on the pavement beside the body. A second paramedic saw me approach and beckoned to me.

'Was it you who called us?' she called out.

Her cheery tone struck me as incongruous, given that we were in the presence of a corpse.

'We just found her,' I explained. 'That is, my dog found her. We were on our way home from the pub and after I called you we went across the road to the tea shop to get out of the cold. My friend owns the place and I work for her, so I have a key.' I paused, realising that I was prattling nervously. Having stumbled on a dead body, I felt oddly afraid, as though I had done something wrong.

'You need to wait for the police,' the paramedic said. 'They're on their way.'

'Police?'

She didn't answer but turned to assist her colleague. A few moments later a doctor arrived, yawning and looking irate. She was kneeling by the body, examining it, when a car drew up and two people stepped out, a man and a woman. The woman took down my contact details and I repeated my account of my discovery.

'Do you recognise the deceased?' the detective enquired impassively.

We were standing under a street lamp and I was uncomfortably aware of her eyes searching my face as she questioned me in her wooden voice.

'Yes. It's – she's – she was –' I stammered. Taking a deep breath, I identified the dead woman as Desirée, the proprietress of the patisserie.

'What is her full name?'

'I don't know. We just knew her as Desirée.'

'We?'

'The village. Everyone who lives here.'

The detective grunted and told me I could go home. As I walked away, I glanced back and saw the two detectives gazing up at the top floor of the patisserie where a window was open, directly above where the body lay. It seemed unlikely that Desirée would have been leaning out of the window for no reason in such freezing weather. I wondered whether she had deliberately jumped to her death, or if she had been pushed.

12

ON SATURDAY, JANE HAD to go out. She was comfortable leaving Holly at her house for a few hours, but I decided to take Poppy to work with me. We had both had a disturbed night. Either she had been unnerved by coming across a human corpse in the street, or she had picked up on my disquiet. Hannah was hoping to be busy in the tea shop with the patisserie closed, and there was no problem if Poppy needed to go outside as the back yard was secure. She often spent time out there, watching birds fly past and sniffing the breeze. If it was raining, she slept in her bed which we kept in the indoor porch by the kitchen door. When we turned onto the High Street, I saw that a forensic tent had been erected across the road, and a cordon was in place on the pavement, meaning that passersby had to walk on our side of the street. In addition, the patisserie was obviously closed, at least for a while. Hannah was excited at the prospect of regaining her customers, even if only temporarily, and she was full of news about the activity outside. She stared at me, agog, when she heard what had happened the previous evening.

'So you actually found the body?' she gasped. 'It was you who found it?'

'Well, it was Poppy really. I would probably have walked straight past without noticing it.'

'And you reported it to the police? Oh my God, if Adam and I hadn't gone the long way round, we might have seen it! What was it like?'

I described the body in as much detail as I could and Hannah hung on my words, open-mouthed.

'It looked like she fell from an upstairs window,' I concluded my account. 'At least, there was a window open up there, and I can't imagine why anyone would want to leave a window open in this weather, especially at night.'

'You don't suppose she jumped?' Hannah asked, echoing my own suspicion.

On reflection, we agreed that was unlikely as the outcome would be uncertain for someone intending to commit suicide. She could have ended up badly injured but alive.

'She could have been pushed,' Hannah added solemnly.

'It's not like you to be in such a dark mood,' I chided her, although the same thought had occurred to me.

No doubt thanks to the closure of the patisserie, we had a stream of customers that morning. Concerned we were going to run out of milk, Hannah asked me to go to the village shop. The walk would give Poppy a chance to stretch her legs. Maud didn't allow large or even medium sized dogs into the shop, due to the packed shelves which made the aisles very narrow. Not only that, but cans and boxes were stacked precariously on every surface. A dog wagging its tail could easily knock numerous items onto the floor. Only dogs small enough to be carried could be taken inside. Lifting Poppy up, I went in.

While her husband was busy delivering Christmas fowl, Maud was comfortably reinstalled behind the till in the grocery store. It was empty when I arrived and Maud came out from behind the counter to greet me with open arms. She was garrulous in her gratitude, waving her hand impatiently at my protestations that she should be thanking Barry, not me. I had barely finished asking about her honeymoon before she launched into a long-winded account of her trip, describing in painstaking detail how she had been searched going through airport security. After that appalling indignity, the flight had been delayed for half an hour. In the course of her recitation, she confided that she had never been abroad before. The flight itself had made a deep impression on her, and she told me how she and Norman had bought chicken salad sandwiches at the airport to eat on the plane. It had been, she said, like a picnic in the air. She giggled, and her joy was contagious. I would have preferred to hear about the honeymoon resort, rather than the flight, every detail of which, according to Maud, had been marvellous. She seemed to attribute the speed and smoothness of the flight to her new husband, and was childishly excited about being given free orange juice on the plane.

'Fresh orange juice,' she explained earnestly. 'Fresh. It wasn't squash. I sell both and, believe me, I can tell the difference.'

Pleased that she seemed happy about her trip, I was relieved that she wasn't quizzing me about the fatal accident that had occurred in the High Street. Probably she had not yet heard that I had been first on the scene. She was eager to carry on talking about her honeymoon, but Hannah was waiting for me. Maud's narrative had barely reached her arrival at her overseas destination when I interrupted her to tell her it was time for me to return to the tea shop. She urged me to stay so she could continue with her account.

'I really should get back,' I insisted. 'Hannah will be wondering what's happened to me.'

'Oh dear, what a pity. You haven't heard the best bit yet,' Maud persisted, visibly disappointed. 'Don't you want to hear about the resort? Norman booked us into the most wonderful place imaginable. It was like a dream. Wait, I'll just show you a few photos so you can see what I mean. There's only forty-seven pictures of the hotel and I can scroll through them quickly. They're all on this new phone Norman bought me. You have to see them. It won't take a moment. You won't believe what the place was like. There were three swimming pools! And our room was like a palace! And wait till you see the breakfast buffet!'

'I really have to go,' I insisted.

'Well, you must come round for dinner one evening, so we can tell you all about it,' she said brightly.

'I'd love that, but right now I need to pick up some milk for Hannah…' I trailed off, seeing her look upset.

'Oh dear,' she said. 'Oh dear. I was afraid this would happen.'

In a low voice, she confided that she had temporarily run out of milk. In the three years I had been living in the village, to my knowledge Maud had never once run out of basic provisions. Even when I had been looking after the shop, we had managed to serve everyone with whatever necessities they wanted. Maud reassured me that she had sent Barry off to the nearest supermarket to restock, but he would not be back for half an hour.

'Possibly longer, if he's needed elsewhere,' she added, with a worried frown. 'This is a disaster, a complete disaster. It wasn't my fault,' she added plaintively. 'I wasn't prepared for this. No one warned me. If people want such a large order, they should let me know in advance. My next delivery isn't due for at least another hour. But what was I supposed to do? This is a shop. I can't turn customers away. If I hadn't given them what they wanted, they might never have come back. People do that, you know. They decide to go into town and stop coming here altogether and she was spending a lot of money here. I was going to offer her a discount.'

'Who?' I had a horrible feeling I knew the answer to my question.

Maud told me that the French woman had been in the previous afternoon, just as Maud was closing, and had bought nearly all the milk in the shop. What was left had been sold that morning.

'What did she want it for?' I asked.

'She said she needed it for some dishes she was creating,' Maud replied mournfully.

'Creating?' I echoed. I didn't add that Desirée wouldn't be creating any more dishes. 'Listen, Hannah's running low on milk at the tea shop. I'll have to nip home and take her whatever I've got. I don't suppose you've got any upstairs?'

Maud shook her head. 'Why don't you wait and see Barry?' she suggested. 'He'll be here soon.' She reached out and held onto my arm. 'Can't you wait? He'll be sorry to have missed you.'

'I'll come back,' I assured her. 'But right now, I need to run. If Barry turns up with more milk, please save a few litres for me. Don't forget, will you?'

'He'll be here soon,' she repeated anxiously. 'He never lets me down.'

It was lucky that Poppy was with me. As though she understood I needed to return to work, she began to wriggle vigorously in my arms, desperately trying to jump down. At the same time, an elderly woman entered the shop. Maud hailed her enthusiastically. As I left the shop, I overheard her launch into details of her marvellous flight. We hurried back to Rosecroft, where I had one litre of milk in the fridge, and returned to the tea shop to find it packed. Hannah was too busy to notice that I had only brought one litre of milk, and I didn't tell her Desirée had bought up nearly the entire stock of milk from the grocery store the previous day. After letting Poppy out into the yard, I hurried to take the orders. We had rigged up a little shelter from the wind for Poppy, knowing how she liked to be outside, and I looked out to check on her every ten minutes or so in case she wanted to come back inside. Almost as soon as we returned, it started to rain. Seeing the first drops fall, Hannah opened the kitchen door for Poppy, who hated to be outside when it was wet. She trotted back in and settled down straightaway in her cushioned basket.

'Did you notice how nice I was to Niles last night?' Hannah asked me, when I went to the kitchen to set out a tray with a pot of tea and half a dozen freshly baked scones which were cooling on a rack in the kitchen. 'I hope you appreciate that was for your benefit, because I know how much you like him.'

'It's not that I like him,' I protested feebly, 'it's just that I remember how hard it was trying to fit in when I was new to the village, so I want to make him feel welcome. I'd do the same for anyone.'

'Yes, I'm sure that's the only reason,' she replied, with a sly grin. 'Look,' she added, her expression suddenly serious as she nodded towards the door. 'Something's going on over there.'

Turning my head, I saw two dark cars parked over the road outside *Patisserie Desirée*. One of them had a blue flashing light.

'It'll be a shame for Niles,' Hannah added, 'but I really hope they close permanently'

We watched from the kitchen door as two strangers climbed out of one of the cars and walked across the road, apparently heading straight for the tea shop. A few seconds later, the bell above the door jangled loudly as they strode in. Their purposeful air suggested they had not come in for tea and cake and a sociable tea break. As I went out to welcome them, the woman held up an identity card and introduced herself as Detective Inspector Dalton, and her companion as Detective Chief Inspector Marsden. She announced that they had come from Swindon to speak to Hannah, who came over and joined us.

My friend looked tense on hearing the ranks of the police officers. This could be no minor civic infringement they were investigating, but a serious crime.

'Has something happened to Adam?' Hannah faltered, turning pale. 'Has he had an accident? Where is he?'

The two detectives exchanged a glance, their expressions inscrutable.

'Who is Adam?' the female officer asked.

'My boyfriend,' Hannah replied, heaving a sigh of relief. 'What's this about?'

For answer, the inspector enquired who I was, before they invited Hannah to accompany them to the police station in Swindon. She protested that she couldn't leave the tea shop, but the detective made it clear she had no choice. A uniformed female police officer materialised, seemingly from nowhere, and ushered Hannah out. DCI Marsden left shortly afterwards and I saw him walk off in the direction of the butcher's and the beauty salon. The inspector who had remained in the tea shop walked over to the door and announced we were closing. Customers who had not finished their tea began to protest, but she ignored them and turned the sign on the door to 'Closed'.

'Can they at least finish their tea?' I bleated, mentally calculating who had been served without yet having paid.

Actually, we were only likely to be out of pocket from two tables. Most customers were still waiting for their orders, since I had been out at the shop when they arrived, meaning service had been slow. No one had complained about having to wait; everyone seemed content to sit watching the activity across the road, even though there was nothing to see beyond a large white forensic tent and a pair of uniformed police officers standing guard at the cordon on either side of it. With a few audible grumbles, and all eyes staring at the detective with undisguised curiosity, the customers gathered their coats and bags and shuffled reluctantly out. I was pleased to see that one couple had left a cash payment on their table. They were regular visitors to the tea shop, and it was heartening to know they didn't blame Hannah for cutting their visit short, and didn't want her to lose money on their account.

Once we were alone, the detective gestured to me to sit down opposite her. Shaking her head when I offered her a mug of tea and a fresh scone, she sat there eying me shrewdly, while I braced myself for whatever was to come, and tried to think of answers to anything she might ask me. But her first question took me completely by surprise.

13

'HOW WELL DO YOU know Chantelle Winters?' the detective asked me.

'Who?'

'Let's not waste time,' she replied briskly. 'Tell me how you met Chantelle Winters.'

Baffled by her question, I shook my head. 'I'm sorry,' I said, 'I don't know anyone called Chantelle Winters. I've never heard that name before now. As far as I know, there's no one called Chantelle Winters living in Ashton Mead. Of course, I don't know everyone who lives here, far from it, so she could live somewhere in the village without my having met her.' I broke off, aware that I was babbling nervously.

It wasn't a good idea to betray that I was feeling irrationally guilty even though I had done nothing wrong. The detective disconcerted me. From her practical short hair to her sensible shoes, she seemed almost robotic, and relentless in her determination to catch me out. With her black eyes locked on mine, she explained that she was asking about the woman who owned the patisserie over the road. She went on to point out that I had reported finding Chantelle Winters' body in the street the previous evening, and had claimed to recognise her when the paramedics had arrived on the scene.

'Oh, you mean Desirée,' I replied at once. 'I'm sorry. I didn't know who you were talking about. Yes, of course I know her. That is to say, I *knew* her. Or rather, I knew who she was, but I can't say I actually *knew* her, not to speak to.'

There was a pause during which the detective sat silently watching me.

'I've seen her a few times from across the road, going in and out of the patisserie,' I carried on, when the silence became uncomfortable. 'And I went there once, or at least I tried to, but she threw me out. What I mean to say is, she asked me to leave. That was the one time I saw her close up while she was alive, and even that was only for a few seconds because I walked out as soon as she asked me to leave.'

The detective tilted her head very slightly and raised one neat eyebrow in a barely perceptible movement as she waited for me to continue.

'That's not what it sounds like,' I said quickly. 'It was all Poppy's fault.' I felt only slightly guilty for blaming the debacle at the patisserie on Poppy. Her barking had, after all, been responsible for what happened. 'She's usually so well behaved, she's never any trouble. You can ask anyone. She's here in the tea shop now, but you wouldn't know it. But for some reason, when we were in the patisserie something upset her and she started making an awful fuss, growling and barking. She made such a racket, Desirée asked me to leave. I can't say I blame her for that, not entirely. Poppy may be small, but she has a really loud bark. The thing is, they hadn't told me at the patisserie that dogs aren't allowed there. There's no sign on the door, and when Poppy walked in with me, no one said a word about it. The waiter didn't bat an eyelid. They should have told me straightaway, before I went in and sat down and placed my order. I never would have taken Poppy with me if I'd known the place wasn't dog friendly. After that, well, I don't know what was bothering her, but something was. Maybe she sensed she wasn't welcome. Actually,' I corrected myself, afraid the detective could tell I was lying, 'it was the waiter. For some reason, Poppy doesn't like him. Whenever she sees him she starts barking. I don't know why. Usually she's very friendly, but she just takes against some people. He probably has a dog at home, and she can smell it on him. It must be something like that for her to bark at him every time we see him.'

The detective nodded. 'So the altercation in the patisserie wasn't premeditated?'

'What do you mean? What altercation?'

The detective stared at me as though she could see right through me. 'You work here, don't you? Did you deliberately set out to cause a scene at the patisserie over the road?'

'Why would I do that? I just told you, Poppy started barking at the waiter, so Desirée asked me to leave.'

She fixed her steely eyes on me again. 'Did you arrange for Poppy to cause a disturbance at the patisserie?'

'Of course not!' The question made me laugh. 'I'm sorry, I shouldn't laugh, but the idea that I could exercise that sort of control over my dog is very funny. Honestly, I wish she *would* do as she's told, but Poppy has a mind of her own. I can't make her follow even the simplest instruction, not unless she wants to.' I sighed. 'She's more likely to do the opposite of what she's told. She's very gentle, and very affectionate, but she's wilful. I tried taking her to puppy training classes but it didn't really help. I suppose you're going to tell me she's spoiled, and – well, you'd be right. I know the police train their dogs to be obedient, but Poppy's not a working dog. Anyway, she certainly wouldn't cause a disturbance on demand. It's taken me long enough to train her to sit when I tell her, and even now she only obeys my commands when she wants to. So I can assure you Poppy and I weren't working together in some kind of conspiracy to cause trouble for Desirée, I mean Chantelle. And even if I could make Poppy start barking like that, why would I want to? The only thing the incident at the patisserie achieved was to make me look as though I can't control my own dog. It was embarrassing for me, but I can't see why it would have done Chantelle any harm.' I shook my head to emphasise my bewilderment at the accusation.

'How old is Poppy?' the detective asked.

'She's nearly four, but I don't see how that can be relevant, because –'

'We decide what is relevant,' she interrupted me brusquely. 'Where's Poppy now? We need to find out what upset her.'

'I wish I knew, but she hasn't told me.' I wasn't trying to be impertinent, but the detective glared coldly at me.

'Murder is no laughing matter,' she rebuked me.

'Murder?' I repeated, astonished. 'Are you saying there's been a murder? In Ashton Mead?'

'I thought you knew.'

'What happened?' I stammered.

'The victim is Chantelle Winters, the woman whose body you reported finding last night, the woman whose patisserie has been taking customers away from this tea shop.' She paused, before adding quietly, 'We have witnesses who heard your friend threaten her'.

I started to protest, but the detective took out a mobile phone and showed me a video of Hannah waving her hands in the air and shouting almost incoherently, 'I'll do whatever it takes to get rid of her and her fancy French pastries'.

'That is Hannah, isn't it?' the detective asked me quietly.

For a moment I was too shocked to speak. 'Surely you can't suspect she was involved in a murder?' I blurted out when I had recovered sufficiently to speak. 'That's impossible. Hannah might have been concerned about the possibility of losing a few customers to the patisserie, but she would never have hurt anyone. She couldn't do anything –'

Just then, Poppy emerged from the kitchen. She ran straight over to the detective and rolled onto her back to have her tummy rubbed.

'This is Poppy,' I said. 'She's trying to make friends with you. You can see for yourself how harmless she is. I admit she can be mischievous, but she's not vicious and she'd never do anything malicious, any more than Hannah would.'

On reflection, I wasn't sure that my claim was altogether true. Poppy understood far more than most people gave her credit for. She was devoted to me, and I wouldn't put it past her to have worked out that the new patisserie was making me miserable. But I kept such thoughts to myself. The police already seemed to think Hannah had a motive for wanting to kill her competitor. It wouldn't help to suggest that Poppy and I had been secretly plotting against Desirée, as though we all regarded her as a serious threat.

'You've got this all wrong about Hannah,' I insisted. 'She might have been annoyed with Desirée for opening over the road from us, but she didn't see her as an enemy. It wasn't like that. If anything, Hannah thought it would help the tea shop to have another café over the road attracting more customers to the High Street.'

The detective stood up without responding. Poker faced, she asked me not to leave the village as the police might want to question me again. I was tempted to ask if she would be wanting to interview Poppy but decided not to be flippant. The detective didn't appear to have a sense of humour and, as she had pointed out, murder was no laughing matter. I had to agree with her on that point, especially when my best friend was being treated as a suspect.

14

HANNAH DIDN'T COME BACK to work that day, nor did she contact me. I thought of phoning Adam to find out if he had any news of her, but with the closure of *Patisserie Desirée*, the tea shop was busy once the detective had departed, and I didn't have a moment to call him. Fortunately, Hannah had been baking over the past week, while the tea shop had been quiet, so we had plenty of scones and cakes. Barry had brought me some milk and I had enough to get me through the day, but I was on my feet from the moment the detective left until closing time, waiting at tables and preparing orders in the kitchen. Doing the work of two people, I pressed on with a determined smile, keen to maintain the illusion that everything was running smoothly and there was no reason to worry about Hannah. If anyone asked after her, I replied cheerfully that she had volunteered to help the police with the inquiry into Desirée's murder. I wasn't sure whether customers believed my story but, convinced that Hannah would be back soon, I didn't want her absence to give rise to any unpleasant rumours about her. Unfortunately for me, we were even busier than before our competitor had opened up. I suspected quite a few local residents were using a visit to the tea shop as an excuse to gawp at the patisserie over the road, no doubt hoping to see some exciting developments. If so, they were disappointed. The forensic tent remained in place, the doors of the patisserie remained firmly closed behind a police cordon, and no one was seen entering or leaving.

According to Barry, the police had sent in a search team, although he didn't know exactly what they were looking for. With Barry unable, or unwilling, to reveal exactly how she had been killed, details of the murder were the sole topic of conversation in the tea shop that afternoon. Behind my back I heard Hannah's name mentioned more than once, but did my best to ignore those conversations. For several hours I was regaled with differing accounts of Desirée's death, each one more dramatic than the last. All of them sounded pretty implausible, and it was quite impossible to imagine Hannah had been involved in any of them. I knew my friend, and had never seen her commit an unkind act, let alone a violent one. According to villagers I spoke to, Desirée had been stabbed or strangled, or poisoned in her own kitchen, before she was thrown out of an upstairs window. No one mentioned to my face who they thought was responsible for the murder, but I suspected many of them thought Hannah was implicated. At times it was difficult to control my temper, and I had to remind myself it was important to continue serving with a smile, and ensure the tea shop kept going until Hannah returned.

'I reckon she paid someone to do it,' I overheard one woman say. She clammed up as soon as she saw me hovering close by with a tray of tea things.

It was a struggle, physically and mentally, to keep the tea shop open, but knowing how worried Hannah was that her future profits would be affected by the arrival of our competitor over the road, I resisted the temptation to close early. By teatime, my mind felt so numb I could barely register the orders. It was a relief when Adam turned up. My arms were stiff from carrying so many trays without a moment's respite, my legs were aching from rushing between the kitchen and the customers, and the soles of my feet felt as though they were burning.

Adam and I had a whispered exchange in the kitchen. He told me he knew that Hannah had been taken to the police station that morning, since he had received a panicky phone call from her asking him to find her a lawyer.

'She hadn't been arrested at that point,' he murmured. 'But she was sure they suspected her of killing the French woman.' He stared at me, his eyes wide with alarm. 'I found her a criminal lawyer, the one my father used when he was in trouble, but goodness only knows how she's bearing up. At least I can tell her the tea shop is coping, thanks to you,' he added, with a tense smile. 'She can count on you, can't she?'

'Of course. If you speak to her, tell her I'm doing what I can,' I replied, trying to sound calm. 'There's a lot to do. I can't keep people waiting. I need to get back out there.'

He nodded. 'That's why I'm here. Tell me what you want me to do.'

After that, we had little time to talk as we were both busy brewing tea, heating up pastries and scones, and serving customers. Adam wasn't accustomed to helping in the kitchen, but he had watched Hannah making tea often enough, and it wasn't difficult putting scones on plates as long as you were careful not to make a mess of the cream and jam. Between the two of us we managed to complete the afternoon service without a hitch. It was the only thing we could do to help Hannah. At last the customers drifted away and, with a sigh of relief, I turned the sign to closed. We cleared up in silence before sitting down with a final cup of tea.

'We have to do something to clear her name,' I said.

'It's absurd to accuse her of murdering that French woman,' Adam fumed. 'Anyone who knows Hannah knows she would never do anything like that. It's just insane. She literally wouldn't harm a fly. She couldn't. I've never seen her acting violently. She hardly ever even loses her temper. She couldn't have done it.'

'Not in a million years,' I agreed. 'It's outrageous the police would even think of suspecting her. It's crazy.'

We gazed helplessly at each other.

'We have to clear her name,' I repeated stubbornly.

'If only we could.'

'We have to.'

'And how do you propose we do that?' he asked fretfully. 'What the hell can we do?'

'If we could find out what time the murder was committed, we might be able to prove she has an alibi for that time,' I suggested hopefully. My voice wobbled as I tried to continue. 'I'm sorry. But honestly, poor Hannah, she's all on her own at the police station. I suppose they're interrogating her and keeping her in a cell, and it's all so unfair. We both know she's innocent.'

Even with Adam's help, the afternoon had been stressful and after we closed the tea shop I went straight home and threw myself on my bed, exhausted, and trying not to think about Hannah. Poppy jumped up and lay on the bed with me, licking my hands as if she understood I needed to be comforted. I was drifting into a doze, when my phone rang. Expecting to hear Adam's voice, I tensed, prepared to hear the latest update and trying not to fear the worst. To my surprise, it was Niles.

'Niles,' I cried out, too tired and emotional after my stressful day to care if I sounded excessively enthusiastic at hearing from him. Recovering my self control, I waited to hear what he had to say. His next words thrilled me.

'Would you like to go out with me?'

I barely managed to control my voice and stop it squeaking with excitement. 'That would be nice,' I said, in as dignified a tone as I could muster, although my heart was thumping so violently I was afraid he would hear it on the other end of the line.

'Perhaps you might leave your dog at home? I was hoping to take you out for dinner at The Plough.'

The bar was dog friendly, but served no food, and there was a large sign in the pub saying that dogs were not allowed in the dining area. I was about to tell Niles that Cliff was happy to turn a blind eye as long as Poppy kept quiet and didn't bother other diners, but then I remembered how she had taken against Niles and barked furiously whenever she saw him. I couldn't risk the mortification of being asked to leave the pub with a noisy dog in tow, and was reluctant to say anything that might cause Niles to change his mind. Once Poppy had grown used to him I knew it wouldn't be a problem, but this was to be our first date and I didn't want to risk offending him by refusing to go anywhere without my dog. She would come to no harm if she was left at home on her own for a few hours. She had brought this on herself by her own behaviour, and had to learn that she couldn't indulge in a frenzy of barking whenever she felt like it. So I agreed to the request and we arranged to meet at The Plough that evening.

There was barely time to shower and change out of my stained work clothes and feed Poppy, before leaving. It felt odd leaving the cottage without her trotting eagerly by my side or, more likely, pulling ahead of me. She didn't usually walk to heel, as my mother liked to point out. However determined I was to train her, this was one point on which Poppy was incorrigible.

'It shows she wants to dominate you,' my mother complained. 'She thinks she's the leader of the pack.'

'When you own a dog, you can lecture me about how Poppy behaves,' I replied sharply, all the more irritated because I knew she was quoting what so-called experts said.

Other than her refusal to walk to heel, Poppy behaved really well, even though I had known nothing about dogs when she arrived in my life. We had learned together, and we hadn't done badly. She rarely took exception to anyone, but now she was being a real nuisance towards Niles. Even so, I felt guilty about leaving her at home on her own, and assured her it wouldn't be for long. Realising I was going out without her, she whimpered and followed me to the front door where she lay down across the welcome mat with her head on her front paws, gazing miserably up at me. I looked down at her, refusing to be guilt-tripped into staying. It was the first time I had been seriously attracted to a man since moving to Ashton Mead, and I was entitled to explore this opportunity. Poppy couldn't tell me in words that I would have to step over her in order to leave, but she might as well have done.

'It's all right,' I reassured her before I left. 'You'll get used to the idea and become friends with him. And I'll never stop loving you. No one can take your place in my life.' Bending down to kiss the top of her head, I left quickly, without looking back at her mournful face.

Niles was already seated at a table in the dining area, waiting for me, when I arrived. There was a large glass of red wine on the table.

'I'm glad you could make it,' he said, smiling, as though my joining him had been in doubt. 'I didn't order a bottle as I wasn't sure if you like red or white, or perhaps you'd like a gin and tonic? Name your poison.' He started at his own expression and looked suddenly grave. 'Some people are saying Chantelle was poisoned,' he added softly, looking shocked.

For a second, I wasn't sure what he was talking about but then remembered that Desirée's real name was Chantelle Winters. It was a slightly unusual combination of French and English sounding names, but I didn't ask him about her. I didn't want to talk about her at all on our first date, but the subject was difficult to avoid.

'It's all been a huge shock,' he said.

Niles told me he had worked with Chantelle in another café, in Paris.

'You lived in Paris?' I enquired, in an effort to shift the focus of the conversation from the dead woman to Niles himself. He interested me more than anything else at that moment.

Appearing gratified by my question, he smiled fleetingly. He told me that when Chantelle had decided to open her own French patisserie in England, she had invited him to accompany her as her manager, since he spoke fluent English. I was pleased to learn that he had been given a relatively senior post. After a few minutes, he himself changed the topic of conversation, saying he was keen to learn about me. I wondered whether he was genuinely interested in me, or if he found the topic of his dead boss upsetting. He asked me all about myself, and appeared to listen attentively to my answers. Already I was imagining him meeting my family at Christmas as my boyfriend, although so far all we had done was meet at the pub for supper together. It would be easier to introduce him to my family as a restaurant manager than a waiter, but that didn't really matter. Whatever his job, I was sure everyone would like him. Even my mother, who was almost impossible to please, was bound to be captivated by him.

It irritated me that my mother had latched on to Barry as a potential partner for me. He had never made a secret of his feelings for me, and he was a reliable man with a steady job. Those were not my main criteria in looking for a partner, but my mother waved my preferences aside with a dismissive air.

'What you want is a man who is honest, hard working, and respectable,' she told me, refusing to believe that I was perfectly happy being single. 'No one wants to be on their own,' she insisted, as though this was an indisputable fact.

'I'm not on my own. I have Poppy, and she's more loyal and reliable than any man,' I countered, 'and a lot less hassle.'

Problems with men were not so easily overcome, as I had discovered through a series of disastrous relationships. I had resigned myself to a single life, and was not unhappy about it. But that was before Niles had come along, offering me new hope of romance.

'No Poppy?' Michelle commented when she came over to take our order.

'I think it's going to take her time to get used to me,' Niles replied breezily, smiling at me as he asked for a bottle of red wine.

'That's a shame. She's usually so friendly,' Michelle said.

'Not always,' I replied firmly, embarrassed for Niles, although he didn't appear bothered by Poppy's hostility. 'She's very possessive,' I muttered.

I wished Michelle would take our orders and buzz off, but she hovered for a few minutes, discussing the menu with Niles, who interrogated her with a knowledgeable air about several of the items. Michelle seemed impressed by his knowledge and, while I was impatient to be left alone with him, I felt a flicker of pride on seeing how she admired him. At last she drifted away and we could talk again. I was slightly disappointed when Niles resumed talking about Chantelle. Although I was curious to hear about the recent murder, it wasn't exactly a romantic topic of conversation.

'She was one of a kind,' he told me. 'They broke the mould when they made her. I can't believe anyone would want to hurt her. Of course, I was with you in the pub when she was killed,' he added, smiling sadly at me. 'Otherwise I might have been there to stop her attacker.'

I was about to point out that since we didn't know exactly when she had been killed, we couldn't be sure we had been together at the precise moment when the murder took place, when he lunged forward and grabbed my hand. He stared into my eyes and I felt my heart pounding when he spoke. 'Emily, Emily, Emily, from the moment I set eyes on you, I've been feeling like I'm on fire.'

'On fire?' I repeated stupidly.

'Yes, on fire, alive, excited, burning with the desire to hold you close. You must know that's how I feel every time we're together.'

We scarcely knew one another, yet Niles told me he had feelings for me, and I assured him that I felt the same way. It was glorious and, at the same time, daunting, because we had only just met.

'We have all the time in the world,' Niles said. 'I thank my lucky stars I came to this village and found you.'

I wished he wouldn't keep talking in clichés but, other than that, he was just about perfect and, like him, I couldn't believe my luck.

15

OUR FOOD ARRIVED, BUT I was hardly aware of what I was eating. Usually, I had supper at home before meeting my friends in the pub for an evening drink. The designated restaurant area of the pub was located on a mezzanine level, which was generally quieter than the bar. The atmosphere higher up felt more sophisticated, partly because Cliff made an effort to make the area look smart, with white tablecloths and linen napkins. Since Michelle had started working there, she had taken to putting little sprigs of flowers on the tables, replacing them in the winter with tiny cacti in colourful pots. These touches combined to create an atmosphere which felt calm, relative to the bar, which was occasionally rather rowdy. As if that wasn't enough to promise an enjoyable evening, having waitress service made me feel spoilt. After spending a day on my feet, ferrying trays of tea and cakes to customers, it was pleasantly indulgent to sit still while drinks and food were brought to us.

Recently, I had been working longer hours than usual, first at Maud's grocery store and then at Hannah's tea shop. In their different ways, both jobs had been more challenging than was comfortable, and I hadn't been sleeping well. As I gazed at Niles across a neatly laid table, my stress and anxiety began to melt away, and I felt myself relaxing for the first time in a while. With a twinge of guilt, I realised it was even a relief not to have to worry about Poppy for a couple of hours.

Niles ordered a second bottle of wine and kept refilling my glass, with a cheery exhortation to drink up. 'We've got another bottle to get through,' he said as we clinked glasses. It was a pleasant wine, and I didn't need much encouragement. What with working so hard recently, and being so tired, not to mention feeling worried about Hannah, I drank too quickly, and was soon feeling lightheaded. We chatted easily about our food, and Niles commented knowledgeably about various dishes. It hadn't occurred to me before to consider Cliff's menu unimaginative, but Niles dismissed it as 'provincial'. When I reproached him for being a culinary snob, he told me that authentic French food was far superior to anything on offer at The Plough. I giggled about frogs legs and snails, but he assured me that French cuisine was far more varied than that.

'You'll be surprised how tasty frogs legs are,' he assured me. 'And snails are quite delicious. All they need is a luscious garlic sauce. You have no idea what you're missing by limiting yourself to an English menu which is, let's face it, pretty pedestrian.' He gestured towards the pub menu which boasted such staples as roast lamb, scampi, and beef and ale pie.

'I'm perfectly happy with this menu,' I protested.

'Ah,' he replied, 'but you are in no position to criticise genuine French cuisine if you have never experienced it. I can assure you French food is far superior to anything you will see on the menu here.'

'What about horse meat?' Michelle muttered, over-hearing our conversation when she came to serve our dessert. She frowned. 'They eat horses in France, don't they?

Niles laughed. 'There's nothing wrong with that, unless you're intolerant of anyone who's not exactly the same as you. Different cultures have different notions about food, that's all. If you allow yourself to be blinkered by narrow minded prejudices against other people's, you'll miss out on all sorts of delicacies. The French are the masters of good taste. You shouldn't dismiss their cuisine in so cavalier a fashion, when you haven't even been to France and tried it.'

There was more along those lines, but I was too tipsy to follow his argument and any movement of my head made the room spin. When he offered to take me to Paris to sample some real French food, I had to be careful not to nod too vigorously. But I had never felt happier. By the time we finished our dessert and left, I was too intoxicated to walk unaided and had to steady myself on the handrail as we went down the stairs to the bar. I descended very slowly and carefully, still sober enough to realise that the stairs posed a challenge. It would be easy to lose my footing and make a spectacle of myself. A tall blonde woman with bright red lipstick was leaning against the bar, watching us as we descended. There seemed to be more steps than I remembered, but at last we reached the bottom and I breathed a silent sigh of relief. The woman looked familiar, although her features were hard to make out. Her lips curled in a smile, but she no longer seemed to be looking directly at me and my answering smile was tentative. Even Cliff had changed from his usual ebullient self. His head had become fuzzy, so that trying to focus on him was like looking at his face through water.

As we reached the bar area, he spoke to me. 'Emily, are you all right?' His features seemed to merge into the optics behind his head, but his voice was clear. He sounded concerned.

'She's pissed,' Michelle said as she flitted past me, leaving a trail of sparkling white light in her wake that made me giggle.

All this time, the woman in red lipstick had been watching me and Niles curiously.

'Who *is* that man she's with?' I heard her ask. 'I don't recall seeing him around here before.'

There was a confused jumble of conversation, and then I was dimly aware that the noise cut off suddenly and I was stumbling along the street beside Niles. As the cold night air stung my cheeks, with a sudden flash of clarity I remembered the identity of the woman at the bar. '*Dana Flack*,' I muttered to myself, naming the inquisitive reporter from the local newspaper, *My Swindon News*. '*I wonder what she's doing in Ashton Mead.*' Dana came to the village when she had been sent to cover a local event, like the May Day celebrations, or the harvest festival marrow competition. The only other time she turned up was when she was ferreting around on her own initiative, sniffing around for a scoop. She seemed to have an instinct for bad news, and I wondered uneasily what had brought her to the village this time.

'Oh dear, I think you need to stop talking and concentrate on staying upright,' Niles told me. 'Let's get you home safely.'

Breathing deeply, I managed to control my legs without too much difficulty. Had I been asked to walk in a straight line, it might have been a challenge, but I had Niles to guide me and we made our way together along the dark streets. He had insisted on seeing me all the way home, claiming I was in no fit state to find my way back unaided. Despite my protestations to the contrary, he was probably right about that. At one point, he grabbed my elbow to stop me tripping over, and I leaned against him for support, nearly knocking him off balance. When he put his arm around me, it felt so natural I could have burst out singing with happiness.

'I'm not altogether sure I didn't start singing,' I admitted to Hannah later.

The journey home seemed to take a long time, but we finally reached my doorstep. Standing beside Niles, I did my best to think only about him, and not about Hannah. Through my drunken haze I realised that worrying about her would make me emotional, and I didn't want to risk embarrassing myself by crying. For some reason, it felt very important that I didn't smudge my mascara. Fumbling to insert my key in the lock, I insisted on Niles coming in, or possibly he was the one who insisted. Whichever it was, I opened the door and Poppy leapt up, growling at him. She had never before sounded so ferocious, except when foxes appeared in our back garden, as they did from time to time. Luckily my next-door neighbour, Richard, had a tolerant disposition, and he was very fond of Poppy, so he never complained about the noise. Whenever I apologised to him, he just laughed and assured me that dogs barked and that was all there was to it. All the same, I never let her out in the garden unsupervised after about ten o'clock for fear of disturbing him at night.

When Poppy was still a puppy, I had been worried the foxes might attack her, but for such a cute friendly little dog, she had a surprisingly loud and fearsome bark. Although the foxes were often fully grown, they invariably scarpered as soon as she started barking at them, and I occasionally saw her chasing a fox that was twice her size. It amused me to see large foxes running away from her, but perhaps they knew she had back-up. I never let her out in the garden unless I was in the house and able to keep an eye on her through a window at the back of the house. Now she barked aggressively at Niles, as though he was a fox intruding on her territory.

Niles drew back, muttering under his breath in French. I wasn't familiar with the phrase, but he was obviously swearing at Poppy.

'It's no use,' I told him, giggling because my words were so slurred. 'She doesn't understand French. They don't teach it in puppy training classes.' I laughed at my own joke, which struck me as hilarious.

'Please keep her away from me,' Niles replied, with an expression that looked more like a grimace than a smile.

His words were polite but his tone was quite frosty, and it made me tremble as it struck me that he might be thinking of leaving.

'Don't mind Poppy,' I reassured him hastily. 'She won't hurt you. She's just trying to defend me.' I crouched down and petted her. 'You're going to have to be nice to Niles,' I warned her solemnly. 'He's my friend.'

Squatting on my heels, I overbalanced and fell sideways, laughing at my own clumsiness; everything amused me when Niles was around. Scrambling to my feet, I grabbed onto him as he helped me up.

'I apologise for Poppy,' I said, slightly sobered by her hostility towards him. 'She's very very protective of me. It's because she loves me,' I added, cunningly giving him his cue to say he could understand why she loved me, or something equally romantic.

Instead, Niles just shrugged. 'Don't look so worried,' he told me. 'A little animal like Poppy doesn't bother me. It's always seemed to me stupid to be scared of dogs that are small enough to be picked up and put outside.' He looked at Poppy as he spoke, and she paused in her frenzy of barking to watch him warily. He laughed. 'She appears to understand me.' He turned to me. 'Perhaps we should go upstairs and shut the door, so we can talk in peace? Come on. Don't bother about that,' he added as I began struggling to remove my coat. 'I'll help you out of it once we're upstairs.'

Poppy whimpered when I told her to stay in the hall, but she seemed to understand she was beaten, and didn't try to follow us upstairs. It felt like the most natural thing in the world to steer Niles towards my bedroom. I had a moment of panic wondering about the state of my bedroom, which was generally a mess, and then even that didn't seem to matter as he closed his eyes and kissed me.

16

I SLEPT SOUNDLY THAT night and woke up early, and alone, with a pounding headache. Niles had gone and Poppy was lying on my bed, licking my hands. I clambered out of bed and showered and dressed, leaving my mobile within reach wherever I was, so I could answer if Hannah called. She had promised to phone me as soon as she was released, but my phone remained obdurately silent. Niles didn't contact me either. He didn't even message me. Only my mother called, wanting to clarify our arrangements for Christmas. It was awkward fending off her questions, but I couldn't confirm what was happening while Hannah's status remained uncertain. For all I knew, she would be in prison on Christmas Day, but I wasn't about to tell my mother that.

After an awkward conversation, my mother rang off, frustrated by what she called my 'deliberately obstructive communication'. I loved my mother, but I did wish she would be more sensitive to my feelings. Forging ahead to establish her expectations for Christmas Day, she didn't once stop to wonder whether there might be a reason for my evasive responses to the questions she fired at me. Had she paused to enquire whether everything was all right, she might even have learned what was happening. As it was, she just succeeded in putting my back up when I was already feeling upset about Hannah, and confused about Niles. Everything in my life seemed to be uncertain. As I hurried out, I noticed that my coat had knocked my spare keys off their usual peg in the hall. They weren't immediately visible among my jumble of shoes so, making a mental note to find them when I returned home, I hurried out.

As though responsive to my mood, the weather was miserable. A sleety rain was falling steadily as Poppy and I set off and she whimpered and clung to my legs until I gave in and carried her most of the way to Jane's house. She hated going out in the rain and for once, I didn't blame her. My old raincoat was barely showerproof. Water leaked through the seam where the hood joined the coat and icy drops slid down the back of my neck and trickled down my spine. Even reaching the shelter of the cosy tea shop and warming my hands on a mug of tea failed to lift my spirits. Apart from the dismal weather, it was strange and depressing having to open up by myself. Hannah and I liked to start the day with a pot of tea and a natter before we opened up. If we had early customers, we would sometimes make do with catching up in the kitchen as we worked. But today the place seemed spookily quiet. Poppy was at Jane's so I didn't even have her company. Alone in the tea shop, I could do nothing but sit and wait, hoping customers would arrive, Hannah would return, and Niles would call me and arrange to see me again. By lunchtime, the rain was still falling outside, and I was still waiting for something to happen.

I tried to cheer myself up thinking about Niles, but we hadn't arranged to meet again. He had managed to convince me that he liked me, and we had seemed to get on really well the previous evening, but I had been drunk. If he had genuinely wanted a relationship with me, in the sober light of day he might have changed his mind having seen me drink too much. Then again, for all I knew, he had only ever been looking for a brief fling and, having once slept with me, he might have lost interest in me anyway. The thought made me feel sick, and I regretted having let him spend the night with me so early in our relationship before we had a chance to get to know one another.

Poppy might present a problem for him, and I was determined to make sure she behaved herself in the future whenever he was around. Much as I loved Poppy, I wasn't going to let her ruin my chances with a man I thought had potential as a boyfriend, possibly even a life partner. With her acute instincts, I convinced myself that, like me, she must have sensed that Niles might become more than a friend. But where she seemed wary, I was optimistic. I liked Niles, and wasn't prepared to walk away from him without a fight.

But even the prospect of seeing Niles again couldn't distract me from worrying about Hannah for long. I was determined to keep the tea shop afloat while she was away, but it was a very quiet day. A couple of customers came into the tea shop in the early afternoon, at the time of the usual lull between lunchtime and tea. This was the busiest we had been all day. I was in the kitchen, brewing their tea and daydreaming, when I heard footsteps approach. For a thrilling instant, I thought Niles had come to see me, and imagined him telling me how he was unable to stay away from me for long. I spun round eagerly to see Barry standing behind me. He wanted to know if I was all right. It was kind of him, but his wasn't the face I was waiting to see.

'I'm fine,' I assured him, doing my best to hide my disappointment. 'I'm not the one you should be worrying about right now. We have to clear Hannah's name. They can't charge her with a crime she didn't commit. She didn't do it. You know it wasn't her.'

'Okay, now you need to calm down.'

'How can I stay calm when Hannah's been accused of murder?'

I didn't tell him that being hungover was doubtless making me more agitated than I might otherwise have been.

'They're just trying to find out what happened,' Barry replied. 'Hannah's not the only suspect.'

'Who else is there?'

He hesitated and looked uneasy. 'You know I can't discuss details of the case with you. I'm not even supposed to know about it myself, as I'm not working on it, strictly speaking. They're only involving me because of my local knowledge. Nothing's clear cut as yet, but Hannah's our friend and –' He broke off with a sigh. 'I just can't believe she would kill someone. Even if she wanted to, I don't think she's capable of it.'

'You have to tell them that, those detectives who are accusing her. You have to convince them they're wrong. You know Hannah. You know she's innocent.'

He shook his head and said his colleagues were only interested in evidence. His opinion wouldn't be enough to convince them Hannah was innocent. So far, the murder weapon had not been found, and until it was, there was no hard proof against any of the suspects.

I repeated my question. 'Who else is a suspect?'

'You know Desirée – I should say Chantelle – and Niles were living together until recently?'

I felt a rush of confusion. 'What do you mean "living together"? They were never in a relationship. They might have worked closely together but there was nothing else between them.'

Barry looked solemn. 'I'm afraid you're wrong about that. They came over here from France together, as a couple, and as far as we know it was a serious relationship, at least for a while. They appear to have split up very recently, so that obviously makes him a suspect.'

'How so?' I asked, struggling not to snap at him, since what he was implying was outrageous.

Just because Niles had worked with Chantelle, that didn't mean they had been romantically involved, and it certainly didn't make him a murderer. Niles had told me he and Chantelle were nothing more than colleagues, and she had offered him the post of manager in her patisserie in England only because he spoke English. Barry seemed to be exaggerating the nature of their relationship because he wanted to put me off Niles. It was unworthy of him.

'The theory is,' Barry went on, 'she dumped him for some reason, and he killed her in a jealous rage. But he insists the split was amicable, and of course my colleagues can't ask her if that's true.'

'If Niles says it was amicable, that should be good enough.'

Barry sniffed. 'Niles claims he was the one who instigated the break up.' He watched me closely as he continued. 'He told the investigating inspector he would have no reason to be angry with Chantelle because he's moved on. He claims he has a new girlfriend.'

My face felt hot and I licked my lips nervously. 'Who?' I murmured, feeling as though I couldn't breathe.

'You,' Barry replied shortly. His voice was flat and his face was totally devoid of expression. Only his eyes glittered with angst as he continued in a low voice. 'You need to be careful, Emily. Niles could be a very dangerous man.' Seeing me about to turn away, he spoke rapidly. 'I'm afraid he's using you for his own ends, and once you've served his purpose, he'll be off without a second thought. And in the meantime, you could be at risk from his violent temper.'

I glared at him, struggling with conflicting emotions. Barry had never made a secret of his feelings for me, but to cast aspersions on Niles out of jealousy was a despicable way to carry on. Too angry to listen to any more of his accusations I told him to leave, before stalking back into the front of the tea shop to serve a new customer and clear a few tables. But I was smiling to myself, because I had my answer and it was official: Niles had told the police we were a couple. My doubts had been groundless, and I couldn't wait to see him that evening. Remembering that Hannah was still in custody, I felt a stab of guilt on catching myself humming a tune as I cleared up at the end of the day.

Perhaps it was because the weather had improved, but Poppy seemed to pick up on my mood and frisked excitedly on our way home, repeatedly darting ahead of me, only to stop to sniff and snuffle in the grass, and then scamper back to trot ahead of me again. Having spent ages trying on and rejecting different outfits, I ended up wearing one of my favourite jumpers to the pub that evening. My clothes decided, I spent longer than usual applying my makeup, followed by a futile attempt to tame my hair. If Poppy hadn't started whimpering to go out, I would have dithered even longer. At last we set off, but my efforts had been pointless, because Niles didn't show up at the pub. Barry was there, and our eyes met a few times, his plaintive, mine hostile. We didn't speak. And then Hannah and Adam walked into the bar, arm in arm. I dashed over and flung my arms around her, Poppy dashing after me to nuzzle her feet in exuberant welcome.

'Why didn't you tell me you'd been released?' I demanded, trying to sound aggrieved but grinning broadly.

She smiled back. 'We thought we'd surprise you all,' she replied. 'They only let me out an hour ago and I just had time to get home and shower before coming here to see everyone. It feels as though I've been away for weeks!'

We sat down with Barry, while Adam went to the bar and Poppy lay down under the table and closed her eyes. Her tail wagged from time to time as she dozed. Hannah didn't appear to have suffered any lasting damage from her night in a police cell.

'It was horrible,' she admitted. 'The worst of it was the smell of the place, all bleach and piss. No, the worst thing was not knowing how long they were going to keep me there. The lawyer was upbeat about it, but until they let you out, you can't rely on anything anyone says.'

Barry began telling us about the laws governing how long a citizen could be retained in custody without being charged, and what evidence was necessary in order to formally charge someone with committing a crime, but Hannah shook her head and turned to me.

'Adam tells me you've been busy in the tea shop.' She smiled at me.

'I wanted everything to be exactly as it was before you went away. Before those bloody idiots started interfering with your life,' I added.

'Well, a smelly police cell isn't my favourite place, but at least I had a rest. It's tough running the tea shop on your own,' she said.

'It was only for a couple of days,' I said, 'and Adam helped.'

'So I don't need to pay you extra for running the place singlehanded,' she teased me, with a grin.

'If you want to pay me extra for managing the place while you were away, I would hate to disappoint you by saying no,' I replied, and we both chuckled.

'Now,' she went on briskly, 'we really need to talk seriously about Christmas. We've wasted far too much time, thanks to my police interview, and it's only just over a month to go until the party!'

We agreed that we all wanted Norman to take on the role of Father Christmas but, with everything that had been going on, no one had yet mentioned it to him. Hannah scolded Barry for not having spoken to Maud about it yet.

'You've had ages to do it,' she pointed out sternly.

Instead of protesting that Maud and Norman had only just returned from their honeymoon, and we had all been preoccupied with worrying about Hannah, Barry hung his head, like a chastened schoolboy.

Barry mumbled that he had been busy, and he hadn't been sure the party was going ahead, given the present circumstances. Normally I would have felt sorry for him, he looked so forlorn. As it was, I was still cross with him and so focused my attention on what Hannah was saying.

'Circumstances?' Hannah repeated sharply. 'What circumstances? What are you talking about? Of course the party's going ahead. You can't cancel Christmas and we don't want to disappoint the village children. The party in the pub is in two weeks time and there's still a lot for us to organise. All *you* have to do is speak to Maud.'

Barry left, promising to go and deal with the situation straightaway, and the conversation moved on to other practical considerations. A small committee of women had been working on the arrangements during Hannah's brief absence. Toys had been ordered and were waiting to be delivered and wrapped, and one of the women had acquired a real sack to hold them. A satisfactorily vast Father Christmas outfit had arrived. All we needed was a few reindeer and a sleigh, Adam joked, and everything would be ready for Santa's visit.

'We could put antlers on Poppy and Holly,' Hannah suggested.

Poppy woke up and let out a bark of protest and we all laughed. Hannah was facing the door, and she looked up with a welcoming smile.

'Here he is, back again.' She glanced at me. 'I knew he wouldn't be able to stay away for long.'

My mood lifted at once and I turned my head, expecting to see Niles but was disappointed.

'Where?' I asked, without thinking.

Hannah looked at me, surprised. Just then Barry joined us and I realised she was talking about him. I said nothing as Barry sat down, grinning.

'Norman's on board,' he announced triumphantly. 'In fact, he's looking forward to it. He's only concerned that the outfit we got might not be large enough for him.' He shrugged. 'He's a big bloke and he looks like he's got even bigger since they went off on their honeymoon. They'll probably be along here later, although I think Maud's more interested in reorganising Norman's house at the moment.' He laughed. 'She's like a pig in shit.'

Hannah assured us all that Norman's girth had been taken into account. A loose costume had been bought in an extra large size. She described it as voluminous, which sounded good enough to me. Barry turned to me and told me quietly that Maud wanted to thank me properly for having helped in the shop while she had been away. She had asked him to invite me to join her and Norman for supper the next day. I wondered if Barry would be joining us, and hoped this wouldn't turn out to be another attempt to push the two of us together. Squirming uncomfortably, I took out my phone to call Maud.

17

OVERNIGHT EVERYTHING SEEMED TO have returned to normal, as though we had all woken from a communal nightmare. It felt like a switch had been flicked. Everything had been fine; life became a nightmare; everything was fine again. Hopefully the switch would not be flicked again, and we could settle back into our comfortable lives, with nothing more stressful to think about than the arrangements for the Christmas period, which was now less than a month away. It was typical of Hannah to want to throw an extravagant party, and there was little anyone else could do to restrain her. When Adam challenged her about the expense, she replied that it was too late to worry about that now. A whole roomful of guests had been invited, and they had all accepted, so the party was going ahead despite his reservations. In the end, we all just went along with her plans. I sometimes wondered how someone usually so composed could be so forceful.

'It'll be fine,' she assured us. 'You'll see. I know what I'm doing.' Her confidence was persuasive, and it was easy to see how she had managed to establish a successful tea shop in the village, through sheer hard work and dogged belief in herself. I could see the doubt in Adam's eyes when he looked at her, and knew he was worried in case her plans ever failed. She was so sure of herself. Meanwhile, Hannah was in her element, baking and preparing. Watching her at work, it was hard to believe that she was still a suspect in a murder enquiry, or that a French patisserie had ever opened its doors across the road from the Sunshine Tea Shoppe. From one side of the tea shop, the patisserie was all but concealed by the village Christmas tree. Only a few spots of pink were visible through the thick branches, and even they were almost lost among the gold fairy lights decorating the tree. Unless you actually looked for evidence that the patisserie was there, it was easy to overlook it.

With Hannah humming happily in the kitchen, and the tea shop packed with our regular customers once more, we settled back into our busy routine. Even the arrival of Dana Flack in the tea shop didn't trouble me. She could sniff around for bad news as much as she liked, but everything was ticking over nicely at the Sunshine Tea Shoppe now that the threat from a rival establishment had been removed. Admittedly the circumstances of the patisserie's demise were regrettable, but the fact remained that the tea shop was now thriving once more. I just needed to see Niles again, and all would be well in my world.

Dana's sharp eyes darted around the room and fixed on each of the few empty chairs in turn. Reaching a decision, she made a beeline for one of the chairs, without waiting for me to offer her a seat. Instead of sitting down at once, she asked the two women at a neighbouring table if she could join them, and shifted the chair to accommodate her at their table without giving them a chance to answer. The two women exchanged an irritated glance, but Dana took her seat and had soon engaged them in fervent but muted discussion. I tried to listen to what she was saying, but it was impossible to hear much above the general din of conversation.

Constantly rushing from the kitchen to the seating area and back again, far from objecting to having to work so hard, I was pleased to know that we were beginning to recoup some of the profit the tea shop had lost over the past couple of weeks. Not only that, but running around was helping me to keep fit. I wondered impatiently where Niles was now, since the patisserie had closed. In my rare idle moments, I couldn't help speculating about whether it might reopen with him in charge.

Even though I could never abandon Hannah and the tea shop, it was exciting to fantasise about what it would be like to work for Niles. Better still, I thought how we might both carry on working for other people until we had saved up enough money to take out a lease on a cake shop of our own. We wouldn't open our fantasy patisserie in Ashton Mead, as we wouldn't want to compete with Hannah, but it would be nearby so we could live together in Rosecroft. In my daydream, Niles was a brilliant pastry chef whose reputation spread rapidly. Together we would establish a patisserie that was unrivalled, patronised by customers who travelled long distances to savour Niles's cakes and pastries. Not content with a single outlet, I imagined us touring the world, establishing successful patisseries in far-flung locations. We would enjoy a glamorous lifestyle together. Niles would create a special dog friendly pastry, in Poppy's honour, and she would travel with us wherever we went, fêted for being our companion.

Lost in extravagant fantasies, I was startled out of my reverie when a sleek Mercedes drew up outside. To my dismay, I recognised the driver and her passenger as they climbed out of the car. With a sinking feeling, I watched the two detectives approach the tea shop and enter, while the bell jangled ominously above the door. I stepped forward and told them we had no free table, but the inspector answered quite curtly that they were not there as customers. They wanted to question Hannah again. I might have asked her to keep her voice down, but it was too late for discretion. Under the watchful eyes of Dana Flack, the male detective strode across to the kitchen from where he emerged a moment later, escorting my friend. Red-faced, Hannah walked quickly across the tea shop, her eyes fixed straight ahead. At least she wasn't handcuffed. A muted muttering spread among the customers as she passed them. Doing my best to ignore Hannah's humiliation, I determined to keep things going for her sake. Serving teas with a bright smile plastered on my face, I tried to ignore the buzz of conversation taking place around me.

'Did you see the look on her face when they took her away?'

'Someone must have done it.'

'That doesn't mean anything.'

'Well, what do you think? Did she do it? Yes or no?'

'You saw them. They as good as arrested her.'

'That wasn't an arrest. She wasn't in handcuffs. They probably just wanted to ask her a few questions.'

'She's already been to the police station three times.'

'Are you sure about that?'

'Maud told me.'

'Oh yes, and you believe everything Maud says.'

'Her nephew's a policeman, so she should know.'

'There's no smoke without fire.'

Observing Dana silently absorbing everything that had happened, and listening attentively to the chatter around her, I was shaken by a cold chill. It was hard enough being left to run the tea shop on my own, at a moment's notice. Being forced to overhear customers gossiping so callously about my friend made it even more difficult. I gritted my teeth and soldiered on. The afternoon seemed to drag on interminably but eventually the last customers asked for their bill. As I was clearing their table, Barry knocked on the door and I unlocked it to let him in. This time, the jangling bell sounded forlorn.

'Well?' I demanded impatiently, as soon as he was inside and the door was locked behind him. 'What's the latest news?'

'I can't stay long,' he replied hurriedly. 'I came here to warn you, they're planning to question you next.'

'Me?'

He nodded. 'They're going to question you here, after you close, to save you having to go to the police station in Swindon. I told them you close at six, so they'll be here any minute now.'

It was an effort to control my panic and thank him. 'What do they want with me?' I asked.

'It's just routine,' Barry assured me. 'Don't worry about it.' But he looked uneasy.

It seemed a funny sort of routine, but there was no point in remonstrating, or asking why he had come to warn me. The fact that he had felt it necessary to prepare me for a visit from the police was enough to persuade me that this could be serious.

'I don't know anything about it,' I mumbled.

'All you have to do is answer their questions truthfully. Once they're satisfied you weren't involved in what happened, they'll leave you alone. The police aren't the villains in all this, Emily. Don't forget that a woman was murdered. The investigation team are just trying to find out what happened. Don't tell them I was here.'

With that, he left. Dismissing a stupid impulse to run home, I settled down to wait. Ten minutes later, at exactly six o'clock, I was busily pretending to wipe tables when the inspector knocked on the door of the tea shop, and I let her in.

'Would you like a cup of tea?' I asked. 'I've just made a pot. We usually brew one when we're clearing up.'

'Thank you. This isn't a social visit,' she replied.

Poppy had other ideas. She ran over to the inspector and rolled on to her back, waving her little legs in the air. For a second, I thought the inspector was going to ignore her friendly advances but then, to my surprise, she leant down and tickled Poppy's exposed belly. Poppy growled with pleasure. My opinion of the inspector changed on the instant. It had taken a dog to make the woman seem human.

'Are you sure you wouldn't like a cup of tea?' I asked her. 'The pot's made and there's more than enough. I'm used to making it for two.'

This time, her refusal seemed less frosty. Straightening up, she began to question me about my relationship with Niles. When I admitted we had only started seeing one another recently, and I didn't know him very well, she turned her attention to Hannah. Some of the questions were easy to answer, like how long I had known my employer, and whether I had ever seen her lose her temper. Others were more tricky. When she asked me whether Hannah was passionate about the tea shop, I suspected she might be trying to catch me out.

'I'm not sure passionate is the right word,' I replied carefully, hoping my prevarication wouldn't give the impression that I was stalling while I thought about what to say. 'Hannah's hard working but I don't think I'd describe her as passionate. Not about the tea shop anyway. Not about anything, really. She's too even tempered.'

'How would you describe her attitude towards the tea shop?' the inspector pressed me, dismissing my attempt to present Hannah as calm and composed.

'I would say she's committed, rather than passionate. I guess you have to be dedicated in any business enterprise, if you want to succeed. It can be challenging in different ways. I mean, we can have a couple of hours when no one comes in, and then suddenly we're packed and rushed off our feet. No two days are the same.'

'She's built this place up by herself, hasn't she?'

'Well, yes, with me to help her. And there's her mother. We all pitch in when she needs us. Hannah's like that. She'll do anything to help other people and people respond to her in the same way. She's a kind person. She gave me a job when I arrived here. Without her generosity and

support, I don't know what would have happened to me.'
I stopped, wary of being too transparent in my attempt to
paint a positive picture of Hannah.

The detective's expression didn't alter but I had a feeling
she was silently assessing my responses, weighing up every
word. It seemed important to appear relaxed, so I poured
myself another cup of tea and tried not to wriggle in my
chair. Seeming to sense my unease, Poppy whimpered.
Seizing the opportunity to escape, I said that my dog
needed to go outside. The inspector gazed thoughtfully at
Poppy, who stared back at her and wagged her tail, looking
adorable. The inspector rose to her feet and thanked me.
As I stood up, I enquired whether Hannah would be able
to go home that evening. The inspector's response was
predictably equivocal. At last, with a final warning that
the police might need to talk to me again, she left. My
ordeal was over, for now. It was time to go to Maud's for
supper, after which my friends and I were going to work
on our plan to help Hannah. I had invited them all to my
house later that evening for a confidential discussion. The
inspector had kept me so late, there was barely time for
me to hurry home to change, and reach Maud's in time
for supper. Quickly I packed some cakes and scones in a
carrier bag for later, locked up the tea shop, and left.

Maud had moved out of her flat above the grocery store
and gone to live with her new husband who owned a
small cottage near the village green. Having lived in her
flat for as long as anyone could remember, it must have
been a wrench for her to move out, but she seemed to have
taken to the change with her characteristic chirpy attitude
to life. Her nephew, Barry, had given up his own rented

apartment in Swindon and taken over the flat above the grocery shop. He had grown up there and it must have been equally strange for him to be living there without Maud, but they both seemed happy with the arrangement. I was curious, never having been invited to Norman's house before. It was a quaint cottage, not dissimilar to Rosecroft, with soft yellow stone walls and a neat garden in the front. It faced onto the village green so it had a pretty outlook at the front, and although I couldn't see it I didn't doubt that Norman tended the back garden well.

'It's lovely here,' I told Maud, as we sat down around a scrubbed wooden table and Norman opened a bottle of wine and poured us each a glass.

'I have plans,' she told me, grinning gleefully. 'Norman's done nothing to the place for years. It's been sadly neglected. But over the summer we'll be busy, won't we, dear?'

Norman let out a deep rich bark of laughter and I thought what a good choice he was to play Father Christmas.

'She's going to have me running around with a can of paint and a brush, climbing up and down ladders and painting everywhere. Can you imagine it? Me, up a ladder!'

'We're just going to spruce the place up,' Maud replied happily. 'And you're not going up any ladders. We've discussed this. Barry's going to help us and he'll do all the climbing that's to be done. I'm not having you falling and hurting yourself.'

'What if Barry falls?' he asked, not unreasonably.

'He won't,' she answered promptly. 'He's young and he's kept himself fit, not like you.'

She glanced at me as she mentioned Barry's fitness and I looked down, wondering if she could possibly have been plotting with my mother.

'And then there's the garden.' She leaned towards me, lowering her voice as though she was confiding a secret. 'I've never had a garden of my own before.'

We discussed how much work a garden was to maintain, and how rewarding it was to enjoy the results of the labour. I suggested she consult my next door neighbour, Richard. While he wouldn't claim to be an expert, he was certainly very interested in his garden and had done a lot of research into different plants. I was beginning to wonder how late I would have to stay, when Maud retreated to the kitchen and returned with plates piled high with pasta, steaming hot and packed with chunks of beef. She had even prepared a plate of meat for Poppy who scoffed it down in no time and came over to me to beg for more.

'We eat a lot of meat, don't we, dear?' she said, smiling at Norman who tucked into his dinner with a loud sigh of contentment. 'Poppy would like it here. Now, I wanted to thank you for being such a help while we were away,' she went on. 'Norman's got his assistant who holds the fort while he's not around, but it's just me in the Village Emporium and I've never had to leave it for a fortnight before. Barry's always been very good, of course, but this was too long a trip for him to cover. So you really were a godsend. I don't know how else I could have managed. Can you believe it? In all the years I've been running the shop, I've never been away for more than a few days.'

'That's dedication for you,' Norman said with a complacent smile. 'You can see why I married her, can't you?'

The dinner was lovely and it was an enjoyable evening in congenial company. For a short while I managed to stop thinking about Hannah and her troubles, but I couldn't forget about her for long. Maud seemed to know that Barry had been invited to a gathering at Rosecroft later on, and she didn't remonstrate when I stood up to leave.

'Would you like a nightcap before you leave?,' Norman asked.

Maud frowned at him. 'Barry and his friends are going round to Emily's,' she said.

Repeating my thanks for a lovely evening, I took my leave. It was nearly time for my friends to arrive and I wanted to be ready for them. Unlike dinner with Maud and Norman, this was not a social gathering. We had serious business to discuss.

18

Poppy wanted to stop and sniff every clump of grass and every patch of weeds on the way home. I felt guilty about hurrying her, but we needed to get back to Rosecroft where I was expecting company. Once we were home, she fussed to go in the back garden so I let her out. When we had first moved in, the fence that belonged to my property was at best rickety and in places completely falling apart, meaning it was impossible to leave Poppy out there on her own. With a road and a river nearby, it had been too dangerous to risk her running off after a squirrel or a bird. Clever as she was, she didn't seem to understand that birds could fly. My neighbour's fence was made of sturdy metal, but the one belonging to my property was wooden and rickety. My staunch friend, Barry, had turned up one day with a set of tools and over a period of several weeks had fixed my fence a few panels at a time. It was uneven, but it was strong enough to keep Poppy safe. Barry described it laughingly as 'a triumph of substance over style'.

Foxes soon began burrowing under the fence, where once they had pushed their way between the wobbly wooden panels. It was easy to block their newly dug tunnels with bricks and, by regular patrolling of the perimeter of the garden, I was able to leave Poppy in the garden unsupervised whenever she wanted to go outside. Occasionally I saw a large fox leap right over the top of the fence, but it was probably too high for Poppy to jump over. She wasn't interested in leaving the garden anyway, clearly regarding it as her territory to guard. She seemed to enjoy running up and down, especially when there were squirrels to chase, and before long she had created her own path through the grass. Curiously, she always seemed to follow the same crooked route across the garden.

While she was outside, sniffing the different scents carried on the wind, on her self-imposed sentry duty against foxes, I popped a tray of scones and pastries in the oven to heat up, and put the kettle on. Having prepared the tea, I wasted precious minutes searching for a corkscrew before I realised the bottle of wine I was planning to offer my guests had a screw top. I arranged the scones and pastries on a plate to cool, hunted for my butter dish and a pot of jam, and was just about ready by the time the doorbell rang. Poppy barked to come inside as soon as she realised we had visitors and she joined Adam, Toby, Barry and me in the living room where she circulated among the guests accepting their attentions with a wagging tail, like a good hostess. She clearly thought they had all come to Rosecroft to stroke her head, scratch her belly, and drop crumbs of scone and cake on the floor for her to hoover up. Apart from Poppy, who was having a lovely time, we were a solemn gathering.

I stared round at my friends. Not for the first time, we agreed that Hannah was blatantly innocent of any wrongdoing, and the police were completely misguided in suspecting her. But we had all said as much before, and our confidence in Hannah did nothing to help her. We were just repeating ourselves pointlessly, complaining about the police.

'Talk about a bunch of blithering idiots,' Adam said furiously, and Toby muttered darkly in agreement. 'They couldn't find a killer if he walked up to them brandishing a machete dripping with blood.'

'Or she,' Barry pointed out gently. 'We don't know the killer was a man. The investigating team seem to think it was possibly a woman,' Barry said.

'They're a menace,' Toby said sourly. 'They're worse than useless, with their random accusations.'

We gazed miserably at one another as I poured the tea, and Poppy whimpered, sensing that none of us was happy. Barry murmured awkwardly that the police were just doing their job, but no one took any notice of him. My next door neighbour, Richard, arrived as I was pouring the tea. While Adam was tall and slender, his father Richard was plump, rosy-cheeked, and short, like a smiling cherub. A retired history professor, Richard had corrected the generally accepted claim that the bridge in Ashton Mead had been built by the Romans. According to Richard, the Romans had probably constructed a bridge on the site of the present one, but the original edifice had long since been destroyed, whether by man or the ravages of time it was impossible to say. As something of an expert in the history of architecture, he was able to assure us that the bridge in its current incarnation dated back to the eighteenth century.

A guidebook of the area referencing the 'ancient Roman bridge that spans the river in the picturesque village of Ashton Mead' had not yet been revised. That same misinformation was faithfully replicated online. Retailers and owners of holiday cottages in and around the village were no doubt happy to suppress the correction, since the bridge was instrumental in attracting tourists to the historic village of Ashton Mead. If people came to see the bridge as the consequence of a misconception, we only had Richard's word for that. On the advice of his friends, Richard was wise enough to refrain from protesting. Village life can be insular, and he didn't want to make enemies. Apart from his unwelcome scholarship, Richard fitted in well, and he was certainly a very affable neighbour. He sat down and enquired after the latest news on Hannah. Adam brought him up to speed in a few words, there having been no developments since he had last spoken to his father that morning.

'We can't sit around and do nothing,' I said firmly but helplessly. 'We have to do something.'

Poppy jumped up, as though eager to start, and Toby smiled. Barry took advantage of the momentary lull in the conversation to point out that, no arrest having been made, Hannah was bound to be released soon. His words offered little comfort to the rest of us. While we appreciated he was trying to be kind, regardless of his reassurances we all knew the police suspected Hannah had done away with her competitor.

'It really is preposterous,' Richard burst out suddenly, his cheeks ruddy with indignation. 'Everyone knows Hannah is completely inoffensive. There's no way she would be involved in anything untoward. It's ridiculous, and frankly it's lazy policing.'

'They're still investigating,' Barry insisted feebly. Clearly he felt obliged to defend his colleagues. 'They haven't reached any conclusions yet.'

'There is only one possible conclusion where Hannah's concerned,' Adam retorted.

Still ignoring Barry's bleating, we proceeded to discuss what we could do to help Hannah. But beyond confirming our commitment to helping her, we still had no ideas.

'Michelle wants to help us,' Toby said. 'She would have been here now, but she had to work.'

We agreed her support could prove useful. Working at the pub, Adam suggested she might overhear something that could help us establish Hannah's innocence.

'She's hardly going to hear someone sitting in the bar confess to murdering that wretched French woman,' Toby pointed out.

'However we manage it, we need to find out who killed Desirée before the police charge Hannah with murder,' I replied. 'Seeing as the police are so useless, we have to get on and do some investigating of our own. We can't sit back and let the police pin this on Hannah just because they can't find anyone else to blame.'

'There is another suspect,' Barry said, with a hesitant glance in my direction.

'Who?' several voices demanded in chorus.

'Her ex, Niles Crawford,' he said.

'What were we saying about lazy policing?' I blurted out. 'He's her ex so he must be guilty. Why don't the police do some proper detective work for a change, and discover who really killed her, instead of jumping to blame her ex-boyfriend? Talk about stereotyping.'

After polishing off Hannah's scones and cakes, washed down with several cups of tea for me and Richard, and beers for Barry, Toby and Adam, we were no closer to thinking of a way to help Hannah. Eventually we agreed to think about the problem overnight. Barry agreed to find out as much as he could from his colleagues on the investigating team, Toby undertook to ask Michelle to listen out for any helpful gossip, and Adam told us he would speak to Hannah and keep us all up to speed with what was going on with her. My friends left. Adam accompanied Toby to the pub, Barry decided to visit Maud and Norman and pump her for any more gossip, and Richard went home. I was too dejected to face having a chat in the pub, and instead settled down on the sofa in front of the television, with Poppy beside me. Only then did I realise how utterly exhausted I was. More than rushing around to keep the tea shop open and our customers happy, my fears for Hannah's wellbeing and safety had drained my energy. There was an old film on the television which I had seen several times before. Poppy fell asleep on my lap. Despite my worries about Hannah, I rested my hand on her side and, to the rhythmic accompaniment of her gentle breathing, I dozed off.

19

I WAS DREAMING WHEN my phone rang, and woke with a start to discover I had fallen asleep on my living room sofa, with Poppy stretched out across my lap. For a few seconds I was too disorientated to work out where we were. Instead of my alarm ringing in the morning, it was Hannah calling to tell me she was home and would see me at the tea shop in the morning. The news was such a relief, it didn't occur to me to complain about her phoning me so late. On the contrary, I felt like celebrating. Instantly awake, and impatient to hear about the latest episode in her run in with the police, I began to fire questions at her, but she was too tired to talk about what had happened. She promised to tell me all about it the following day, and I had to be content to wait until the morning. That night, I could barely sleep for excitement, knowing we would be working together again in the tea shop the next day. Hopefully the police would leave her alone from now on. That said, we would only be able to catch up in the intervals between serving customers. Although we both liked to keep busy, and despite the fact that Hannah was keen to make up for her recent losses, I secretly hoped for a quiet day in the tea shop, with hardly any customers.

The following morning I was up early, eager to get to work. When I dropped Poppy off at Jane's, we hugged and congratulated each other as though we were personally responsible for Hannah's release. Leaving Poppy snuggling down beside Holly for a nap, I made my way to the tea shop where Hannah greeted me with a huge grin, a pot of tea and a batch of fresh scones. All of the crockery at the tea shop was pretty, but Hannah had deliberately bought individual cups and plates, rather than co-ordinating sets. She assured me that, far from being unique, her diverse choices displayed an established style known as mix and match. However she had come by the idea, it worked, and in a traditional village like Ashton Mead, her mismatched tea sets looked not only decorative but also quirky and slightly audacious.

As we sipped tea from our different cups, mine a delicate white porcelain decorated with pink roses, Hannah's pale green with yellow rings, she confided that the police still regarded her as a suspect. It seemed they were too dim to understand there was a reason why they could find no evidence against her. I wondered whether the police could really be that stupid, or was it possible they knew more about Hannah than I did, and my blind trust in her was naïve? Just for an instant, I struggled to dismiss my suspicions, and despised myself for doubting her. But there was no time to dwell on police incompetence, or worry about my own misgivings. It was nearly the end of November, and we still had a lot to organise. Getting on for twenty people would be gathering at the Sunshine

Tea Shoppe for lunch on Christmas Day, and Hannah was determined to serve a traditional Christmas lunch, with all the trimmings. In a brief interval of quiet, we listed the people we had invited and I scribbled the names down. It didn't surprise me that they had all accepted Hannah's invitation. Everyone knew her cooking was sensational. There were seventeen names on our list so far: Hannah, Jane, Emily, mum, dad, Susie + family, Adam, Richard + family, Toby, Michelle, Naomi, Maud, Norman, Barry.

Hannah suggested we cater for twenty, as she said it was better to be over-generous with provisions than risk running out, and any leftovers would not go to waste. It would also allow us to accommodate any unexpected additions to our party. Since she was doing most of the preparation and cooking, I deferred to her judgement without questioning it.

'People tend to overeat on Christmas Day,' she said and I agreed, thinking of my teenage nephew who could eat enough for three and still want more.

There was one other name I was keen to add to our list. It would have to be a last-minute invitation, but I knew Hannah wouldn't mind that. Uncertain of my relationship with Niles, I wasn't sure how to invite him, but was hoping we would spend Christmas Day together as a couple. Since Barry had let slip that Niles had called me his girlfriend, we hadn't seen one another. Evidently he was keeping a low profile. With the police looking into his ex-girlfriend's death, he was probably wise to avoid drawing attention to himself. I tried not to fret, although it was a week since we had gone out together. From the tea shop, I kept a determined eye on the patisserie over the road, but saw no one going in or out. Once I thought I caught sight of him walking past and nearly cried out, but then the figure turned and I saw it was a stranger who resembled Niles vaguely from the back.

In desperation, I wondered if Barry might be able to help me, but thought better of asking him. There was no guarantee Barry would be prepared to pass on any information, even if he knew where to find Niles. Reluctant to admit that I didn't even have an address for Niles, I decided against asking anyone else for help. I was afraid I had misread the signs and our brief fling was already over, before it had really had a chance to begin. The problem was doubtless the disastrous timing of our meeting. Following the horrific death of his boss – who, according to Barry, had also turned out to be his ex-girlfriend – embarking on a new relationship was probably the last thing on Niles's mind. His life must be complicated enough already, and his emotions must be in turmoil. In the end, my only sensible option seemed to be to dismiss Niles as a lost opportunity, and try to forget about him.

Making such a resolution was one thing. Keeping it was another matter entirely. I tried to convince myself that Poppy was better company than a boyfriend and, in many ways, that was true. Poppy made no demands on me, except to be taken for walks as frequently as possible, which benefited me as well. Other than that, as long as she was fed she asked for nothing but love, which she returned with an unconditional and unwavering devotion. I had only to pet her and she was content.

'If humans were as easy to please as you are, the world would be a much happier place,' I told her, and she wagged her tail.

After work on Saturday, I went home to change and grab a bite to eat before going to the pub. Hannah, Adam, Toby and Barry were sitting around a table when I arrived. Leaving Poppy with them, I went over to the bar and waited to be served. Michelle seemed to be pulling pints and pouring spirits really slowly, but at last she reached me. As she was putting a glass down in front of me, I noticed a familiar aftershave and turned to see Niles standing beside me. Stifling a squeal of elation, I smiled at him. Accepting my offer to buy him a drink, he leaned over to peck me on the cheek. Suddenly my face felt burning hot, and I looked away to hide my blush. A moment later, armed with our pints, we made our way over to join my friends.

'What are you doing on Christmas Day?' I asked him.

He shrugged, careful not to spill his drink. As we drew near to my friends, Poppy snarled ferociously. Putting my glass on the table, I bent down and picked her up. Holding her tightly, I scolded her for her bad manners and she hung her head. Chastened but not cowed, she continued growling very quietly without taking her eyes off him. Niles ignored her and smiled as though nothing was amiss. She began wriggling to get down.

'I'll put you down,' I warned her, 'but only if you behave. Poppy, no barking.'

She retreated under the table, whimpering.

'Is it okay if Niles joins us on Christmas Day?' I asked Hannah, who gave me a knowing grin.

'Yes, we'd love to join you, wouldn't we, Emily?' Niles said, and I smiled to hear him talking proprietorially about me, as though we were an established couple.

The conversation moved on. Adam warned us that snow had been forecast for Christmas Day. Cliff overheard us discussing whether that was likely, the weather having been so mild lately. We divided into two camps, those who were sure it would snow on the twenty-fifth, and those of us who were equally convinced the bad weather would hold off until at least the twenty-sixth. Niles didn't stay long, but I wasn't too disappointed, because we were going to spend Christmas Day together, and he had made it clear he wanted to be with me. Even the prospect of introducing him to my mother no longer seemed daunting.

20

ON THE MORNING OF the children's party, I looked out through my bedroom window at a grey and ominous sky. Even though it was nearly a week into December, the milder weather had held until now. It would be disappointing if the weather turned just on the day of the party. After a warming bowl of porridge, I decided to wear an extra fleece under my coat and Poppy let me put on her little red jumper. When we were both suitably wrapped up, I put Poppy's lead on and we left the cottage. A bitter wind was blowing when we stepped outside, and it felt cold enough to snow. We set off at a brisk pace, past crisp blades of frosty grass, under a louring sky. At first Poppy trotted quickly in front of me, but she was soon stopping to sniff the ground, seeming oblivious to the freezing conditions. I urged her to hurry, before my fingers and toes started to hurt, but she kept discovering little patches of ice that excited her curiosity. It seemed to take us a long time to reach the tea shop and, for once, I was quite pleased not to be taking her all the way to Jane's house.

Jane was already at the tea shop with Hannah when we arrived, helping with the preparations for the party.

Hannah had closed early and together we set off for the pub where we helped move the tables out of the way to make room for the children to queue up to see Father Christmas.

'This is going to be fun,' Hannah said.

I knew she was trying to focus on the Christmas parties to distract herself from her troubles with the police.

'I wish we hadn't invited Barry,' I said, once we had finished organising the room.

Hannah sat down beside me with a sigh. 'Why?' she asked me. 'What's he done now?'

I explained how he had been determined to put me on my guard against Niles, just because he was jealous.

'According to Barry, Niles is taking advantage of me and he's a dangerous man,' I scoffed. 'How pathetic is that? It's obvious he's only saying it because I prefer Niles to him.'

'What if Barry's saying it because it's true?' Hannah asked. 'He is a policeman, after all, and he must know things we don't hear anything about.'

Before I could remonstrate, Cliff came over with a plate of cupcakes taken from the supply which Hannah had brought over for the children's party. Jane joined us and she and Hannah became engrossed in discussing turkey and vegetables, and whether one or both of them should bring their microwaves to the tea shop early on Christmas Day and, if so, how they might most easily transport them. My sister and her family were arriving on Christmas morning, and my parents had arranged to stay with me on Christmas Eve. I was excited about seeing all my family, but not looking forward to tidying up Rosecroft. I would have to make sure I had fresh sheets for the spare room, and check that the house was clean and tidy. In the meantime, we had the children's party to get through.

We were ready, the children were due, a sack of presents was safely concealed behind the bar, and all we needed was for Father Christmas to be in place before the children arrived.

Cliff brought over a tray of mulled wine. 'This might be a children's party, but adults are allowed to enjoy themselves as well,' he said. 'You've done all the hard work, preparing, now you can relax and enjoy yourselves.'

As we were raising our glasses, we heard a cacophony of shrill voices outside. The children who lived in the village had arrived, accompanied by several parents and one of their teachers, Alice. I knew Alice vaguely, having met her in the pub a few times. She was the only one of the local teachers to live right in the centre of the village, not far from the pub. As soon as the children arrived, rosy-cheeked and shrieking with excitement, she looked as though she regretted her decision to attend the party. Alternately laughing that this was a busman's holiday for her, and expressing dismay that none of her colleagues had come to help out, she seized a glass of mulled wine from a tray Michelle was handing round to the adults. Alice had wound her hair into a neat little brown bun at the nape of her neck and it bobbed up and down as she gulped her drink.

'Down the hatch! I hope you haven't boiled off all the alcohol,' she chuckled, looking a trifle frantic.

The children started pestering Alice, wanting to know where Santa was. She assured them he was on his way, and hurried to the bar to replenish her glass. This time, I noticed she added a tot of brandy to her mulled wine. It was going to be a long afternoon.

Maud arrived with Barry and they assured us Norman would be with us very soon. They had left him putting the finishing touches to his outfit. Maud had come on ahead with Barry, to make sure the children were primed and waiting. Since she had married Norman, Maud had mellowed. No longer an avid gossip, she had stopped obsessively prying into other people's business and had become quite serene. Hannah and I both wondered how long the transformation would last. Maud was soon busy telling Alice all about her honeymoon.

Barry drew me to one side to enquire quietly where he might find Niles. I answered breezily that he would be joining us on Christmas Day.

'That's nearly three weeks away,' Barry said.

'Yes, well, he'll probably be here later. He knows I'm here,' I added complacently.

'Tell me where he is right now,' Barry insisted, gripping my arm and looking worried. 'It's really important you tell me where he is.'

Pulling myself free from his grasp, I replied coldly that I had no idea where Niles was just then. 'I know you don't like me seeing him,' I added in an angry undertone, 'but you might as well get used to it.' With that, I turned and flounced away.

'Wait, there's something I have to tell you,' Barry called after me.

Unwilling to hear more slurs against my boyfriend, I hurried to the bar, where Alice was knocking back another brandy. This time she hadn't bothered to conceal it in a glass of mulled wine. Moving sinuously across the floor, Dana Flack approached Alice and began to chat. I wanted to warn the unsuspecting teacher to be discreet, because in my experience there was always a hidden agenda behind Dana's questions, but it was too late. The two of them were already engrossed in conversation, and Dana was signalling to Michelle to bring Alice another shot of brandy.

'I shouldn't, really,' Alice was saying as I walked past.

'It's nearly Christmas,' Dana replied brightly. 'And anyway, it's the weekend. You're not at work now.'

We didn't notice exactly when the snow began to fall. A little girl shrieked, 'Snow!' and the other children scuttled to the window to look out. Over their heads we saw huge flakes swirling thickly around. Within a few moments it was settling on the road and the pavements were almost swallowed in a layer of snow.

'I hope the other children manage to get here,' Hannah said.

'The outliers won't make it,' Cliff announced with a prosaic shrug. 'Take it from me, the roads'll be closed before long. It's the hill into the village that's the problem in bad weather,' he added by way of explanation.

'Oh dear,' Michelle said. 'Oh dear, oh dear. Is everyone going to have to spend the night in the pub?'

We all hastened to reassure her that the snow was not heavy and we would be able to get around quite easily as long as we were careful not to slip over. In a heavy snowfall, the geography of the place made arriving and leaving difficult; in a blizzard it would be almost impossible. But the weather hadn't been as bad as that for a few years. If it did deteriorate, we might be cut off until the snow ploughs got through. I hoped the weather wouldn't deter my parents from joining us, but there were still nearly three weeks until Christmas Day, and the weather might improve by then. Meanwhile, the children were growing impatient, shut up indoors while outside the snow fell thickly, perfect for making snowmen and snowballs. Our plan had been that Norman would arrive and be in place, waiting for the children to arrive. They were to line up in an orderly fashion, receive their gifts, have a glass of orange squash and a biscuit, and go home. But the most detailed of plans can go awry. Now we were faced with a gang of rowdy children, and nothing for them to do but whine and yell to go outside and play in the snow which was now falling with alarming heaviness, obscuring the sky and shrouding most of the street in brilliant white.

Cliff decided to hand out biscuits and orange squash to the waiting children.

'Line up! Line up!' he shouted.

'He doesn't have any children, does he?' Alice wailed, her voice slurred.

'They're going to be hyper after all that sugar.'

'Aren't they already hyper with excitement?' Michelle asked.

Alice let out a sound that was either a laugh or a groan. It was impossible to tell which. She seemed unaware that her neat bun had come undone and her hair now hung over her shoulders in a tangled mess. Leaving her in charge of the children who were all clamouring to go outside and have a snowball fight, or badgering her to tell them when

Santa would arrive, Barry gathered the adults together in one corner. He looked very solemn.

'The results of the forensic tests from the victim's lodgings above the patisserie have come in,' he announced solemnly. 'I'm sorry to have to tell you that there is no longer any doubt about the identity of Chantelle's killer.' He paused for breath.

'Surely that's a good thing?' Michelle whispered.

Adam gripped Hannah's hand, his expression fraught, while she stared at Barry as though transfixed.

'The killer,' he announced in a subdued tone, 'is Niles. We need to find him before he can harm anyone else.' He looked at me, stricken, and I dropped my gaze, unable to meet his eye.

I could feel myself shaking, but couldn't tell whether it was shock or fury making me tremble.

'He knows we're looking for him, and we will find him,' Barry continued, sounding more confident. 'We suspect he was planning to slip away under cover of darkness, but the snow might have scuppered his plans. If anyone sees him, do not approach him. He is a very dangerous man. He has a history of violence and has already killed once, at least.' He turned to me. 'I'm sorry, but the evidence is irrefutable. We have to find him before he does any more harm. We know him to be a reckless criminal, who has taken advantage of women in the past, and he will be desperate. So please, everyone, be on your guard. As far as we know, he's not left the village yet. He could be hiding out anywhere.'

He wasn't looking at me as he said that, but I knew he was talking to me. Maud covered her mouth with one hand and let out a squeal of dismay.

'Don't worry,' Barry reassured us. 'We have officers ready to swoop in and search the village as soon as the roads are clear.'

'At which point he'll be able to make his escape,' Adam pointed out gruffly.

'At least he won't be prowling around here anymore,' one of the mothers said.

As a buzz of muted conversation broke out among the listeners, there was a shriek of excitement from across the room, and the children all began gabbling and giggling, their voices rising to a crescendo until we couldn't hear each other speak.

'Boys and girls, be quiet!' Alice's howl floated helplessly across the bar, barely audible above the racket.

The children took no notice of her. Their attention was focused on Father Christmas who had been spotted outside.

21

BY NOW THE CHILDREN were jumping up and down and screeching with glee. Alice clutched her brandy glass in front of her like a shield, and exhorted them to be quiet, warning them that Santa Claus wouldn't come in while they were making so much noise. Her words went unheeded and a moment later, the door opened and Father Christmas entered, shaking snowflakes from his cloak. His hat was covered in melting snow but he left that on, even though his head must have been cold. Keeping his hands on his hips underneath his cloak, which spread out around him like a cumbersome tent, he stared around, his face concealed in cotton wool. The children fell back, and a sudden hush descended. One little girl with long blonde pigtails stepped forward, her eyes screwed up suspiciously.

'Where ith your thack?' she lisped. She turned to Alice and tugged her hand. 'Where ith hith thack?'

'Hith thack?' Cliff repeated, looking baffled. 'What's she talking about?'

'The one with our prethenth?' the little girl exclaimed, stamping her foot impatiently.

The other children took up the cry, chanting in a ragged chorus, 'Where's his sack?' and 'Where's our presents?'

As if the children weren't making enough noise, their exuberant cries started Poppy yapping, and I picked her up and murmured in her ear. Usually a firm instruction to stop barking was enough to calm her, but she was too agitated to settle down. While I was trying to persuade Poppy to be quiet, Cliff winked and whispered to Michelle who started pouring more mulled wine while he ducked down behind the bar.

'It's here,' he hissed, beckoning Norman, who was still gazing around as though uncertain what to do. 'You're supposed to collect it from behind the bar, remember?'

Cliff cast a frantic glance at Maud who was fast asleep, knocked out by the excitement of the day. A brandy, or possibly two, had finished her off and she was slumped on a chair, snoring gently.

'She told me she reminded Norman only this morning,' Hannah muttered.

Meanwhile, Cliff was grumbling loudly enough for everyone to hear. 'You know what to do, Norman. Get on with it! Come and get the bag, and don't let the children see what you're doing. Remember, you're supposed to have brought it with you on your sleigh,' he added in a fierce whisper. Heaving an exaggerated sigh, he held a bulging sack up and glared at Norman, while Barry gave the dithering Santa a shove, trying to propel him towards the bar.

'The reindeer left this here for you, Santa!' Cliff bellowed, as a few children peered suspiciously over the top of the bar.

'You mean the elveth,' the little girl corrected him waspishly.

'It's a pity Cliff refused to be Santa,' Hannah whispered to me. 'Norman's like a rabbit in the headlights faced with all these children.'

To be fair to Norman, the children were quite intimidating. There were about twenty of them, of varying sizes and appearances. A couple of the older boys were tall and stocky enough to be teenagers, and they stood glaring at Norman like thugs who had been let loose on the world prematurely, and there were a handful of girls who looked far too old to believe in Father Christmas. The remainder of the cohort were smaller, and ranged from about ten to maybe three years old. Some of the youngest ones stared at Norman, wide-eyed, but most of the children were focused on the large sack which Cliff had heaved onto the top of the bar where it lay, precariously balanced, and bulging with wrapped toys.

'Here you are, Santa,' Cliff yelled. 'The elves left this here for you.'

Norman shuffled over to the bar and grabbed hold of the sack.

'Don't spill them!' Cliff cried out, huffing with frustration at Norman's ineptitude.

'Why did he agree to do it if he wasn't up to it?' Michelle muttered audibly.

'The Bargain Store in Swindon is brilliant,' Alice announced to no one in particular. 'Just brilliant. I was on the committee. The children's gift committee.' She hiccuped.

'Have another brandy,' Cliff said wearily. 'This one's on the house.'

'More mulled wine anyone?' Michelle called out.

'Did he come down the chimberley?' an impish little boy asked, provoking a spate of scathing comments from the assembled children.

'How could he get that sack down the chimbley?'

'Well, he didn't have to because the elves left it here.'

'He's too fat to come down the chimney.'

'You'd be fat if you had to eat a mince pie in every house in the whole world.'

'Only the houses where there are children.'

'All houses have children.'

'My gran hasn't got any children in her house and Father Christmas comes down *her* chimney. She sees him every year.'

'You're silly. He only goes to houses where children live. Everyone knows that.'

'He only goes to the houses where the children are *good*.'

'Shall we get on with it?' Norman snapped gruffly. He didn't sound very jolly. At the sound of his irate voice the children stopped chattering. 'Ho ho ho, children,' Norman added halfheartedly.

Alice seemed to recover from her drunken haze and began organising the children into a line. 'The sooner you're quiet, the sooner we'll all be able to go home and lie down – what I mean to say is, once everyone is quiet, you'll be getting your presents,' she said, attempting to sound bright and cheerful. 'Come on, now, line up nicely for Santa. He's come all the way from Lapland.'

'Where are your reindeer?' one of the boys asked.

Santa didn't answer. He rummaged in the sack as the first child in the queue shuffled forward to receive a present wrapped in red paper. The girl held out her hand, but Alice ran forward and asked her to wait in line a moment longer.

'Santa's not ready yet,' she told the child.

She turned unsteadily to face Norman and whispered loudly. 'Remember, it's green for the girls, and red for the boys. It couldn't be simpler. Green for boys, red for girls. Please get it right. And don't forget to ask them if they've been good. And don't worry about the naughty ones, they'll all say they've been good anyway. And you might say "Ho ho ho" and try to sound jolly,' she added plaintively.

While all this was happening, Poppy was whimpering in my arms, wriggling and growling at me, trying to jump down. Abandoned by Maud, Barry came and stood beside me. The children were growing fractious and starting to run around, chasing one another and knocking chairs over. Cliff decided it was time for Santa to start giving out presents, while Michelle handed round more mulled wine to the adults.

'This is a party!' Cliff shouted angrily. 'A party for the children! Come on Santa, let's hand out those presents!'

As he was speaking, Cliff pulled on a red Father Christmas hat and began shaking his head to make the white bobble bounce around as he instructed the children to form a queue. 'Line up, line up, children. A present for everyone, ho ho ho,' he called out.

'You're not Santa,' a small girl objected, but the rest of the children seemed happy enough to queue up for their presents.

They fidgeted as they waited, and then the first small girl approached Norman's chair, her expression a mask of terror.

'Go on,' the little girl's mother urged her. 'Don't be scared. It's Santa. He's got a present for you.'

Father Christmas suddenly bellowed 'Ho ho ho' so loudly it made the little girl cry. She ran to her mother, and a boy stepped forward.

'And what's your name?' we heard Norman enquire in an unnaturally deep voice he was putting on for the occasion.

Without warning, Poppy sprang from my arms and launched herself at the child who fell to one side, bawling. Momentarily immobilised with shock, I watched in silence as the boy scrambled to his feet.

'Get that brute away from my son!' a voice roared.

Ignoring my frantic summons, Poppy pushed past the crying child and seized Santa's beard in her teeth.

'Get off me!' Norman yelled, waving his arms around. He whacked Poppy on the head, but she clung to his beard as he struggled to his feet.

For a moment Poppy hung on, suspended above the ground, then she slithered down his chest and fell to the floor. Had her claws not dug into the loose fabric of his costume and slowed her descent, she might have been seriously injured. Her fall was also slowed by the fake beard, which remained firmly gripped in her jaws and pulled away from its fastenings slowly. As the fake beard and whiskers were ripped from his face, we were astonished to see Niles staring at us. If it was startling to watch his Father Christmas disguise torn off, it was even more shocking to see his face without its customary mask of dazzling charm. His lips twisted in rage, and his eyes darted savagely around, like a cornered rat.

'Niles!' Cliff cried out. 'What the hell are you doing in that costume?'

'I had to get away,' Niles panted, still glaring around. 'It was the only way.'

Barry started towards him, his progress hindered by the dispersing group of children, but Niles was too fast for him. He spun on his heel and made for the door. Poppy threw me a fleeting glance, a quizzical expression on her face, as though requesting permission to pursue the fleeing figure.

'Go on, Poppy!' I shouted without thinking, and she sprang after Niles, who had nearly reached the door.

'Follow his footprints in the snow when he gets outside!' one of the children screeched excitedly.

The other children took up the cry to follow Santa's footprints.

'Is he going to Lapland?' a shrill voice asked. 'Can we go there, mummy? Please? I promise to be good.'

22

EVEN IF HE HADN'T been hindered by his costume, Niles would have been no match for Poppy's speed. She reached him in a couple of bounds, before he made it to the door. She must have sunk her teeth into his ankle, because he let out a blood-curdling shriek. Poppy had never bitten anyone before, and I sensed her weeks of pent-up frustration at being restrained from attacking him. Niles continued to yell and managed to shake her off, so that she dropped to the floor. She had stopped him for a few seconds, just long enough for me to draw level with him. I leapt forward to grab her and pull her out of his reach, but my foot slipped on the hem of his red cloak and I landed on the floor. Niles was on top of me in a flash and before I could drag myself away from him, he grabbed me around the throat and yanked me to my feet.

'Get back!' he yelled, struggling to remove his Father Christmas outfit without loosening his grip on me. Abandoning his attempt to free himself from his scarlet costume, he drew out a knife that had been concealed somewhere beneath its voluminous folds. 'Get back or

I'll kill her!' he shouted, pressing the point of the blade against the side of my neck.

There was a sudden silence. No one spoke. No one dared move. There was no longer any doubt in anyone's mind that Niles had murdered Chantelle. We had no reason to suppose he would hesitate to do the same to me, if he was desperate enough, and the look in his eyes was maniacal. I tried to be brave, but trembled, feeling the point of Niles's knife pressing against my skin. Closing my eyes, I stood perfectly still, pretending none of this was happening and silently praying that he would let me go. My thoughts raced, wondering how to break his hold on me but when I shifted, his grip on my throat tightened and the point of the knife pricked my flesh.

Barry broke the silence. 'What do you want?' he asked, sounding unbelievably calm and reasonable, as though this was some everyday transaction being worked out between friends. 'You know you won't gain anything by harming Emily. As long as she's unhurt you won't get yourself into any worse trouble, and you can use her as a bargaining chip.'

He was careful to suggest I might be hurt, rather than killed, but his words made me shudder and I moaned softly. Nearby, I heard Poppy whimper but she seemed to understand that she was powerless to help me.

Barry continued. 'Why else did you grab hold of her, if not to help you get whatever it is you want, on your own terms. Nothing else makes sense, and you're no fool.'

Niles's grip on my throat loosened slightly, and I began to hope Barry knew what he was doing.

'Negotiating with us must be your priority, if you are

going to walk away from here a free man,' Barry went on, in a conversational tone. I wondered how he managed to sound so relaxed when I was in the grip of a psychopath. 'None of us wants to stand here like this indefinitely, in this impasse. So tell us what you want and we can start to work out what to do. I take it you do have an exit plan?'

There was a pause during which no one spoke. I opened my eyes and looked around. Barry was standing in front of everyone else. At a first glance he looked perfectly relaxed, yet he was unnaturally still. Cliff was standing behind the bar with Michelle and Toby. The three of them were motionless, staring at me, their faces pale with terror. Adam was clutching Poppy to his chest. One hand holding her jaws shut, he ignored her frantic wriggling as she tried to free herself from his grasp. All the adults were staring, aghast, seemingly incapable of movement. Only the children displayed any signs of animation. A little girl burst into tears, wailing that Father Christmas hadn't given her a present, while her mother whispered to her, in a vain attempt to keep her quiet. A few small boys were grinning exuberantly. Only the older children looked on solemnly, suspecting that the party was not going to plan.

'What do you want us to do for you, in exchange for your letting Emily go unharmed?' Barry asked. 'You can have whatever it is you want, as long as you let her go.'

Niles tightened his grip on my neck again, yelling that he didn't trust Barry. Meanwhile, Poppy was watching what was going on, her eyes bright with concern.

'Let her go,' Barry repeated quietly.

Poppy let out a muffled bark, as though she thought Barry was exhorting Adam to release *her*.

'Keep that vicious brute away from me. If it tries to attack me again, you'll be sorry,' Niles snarled, jerking me so that I nearly lost my footing.

By now he had wound his arm around my neck, pressing the side of his hand against my throat until I could scarcely breathe. Keeping tight hold of me, he began to edge backwards towards the door. I groaned. He reached behind him to push the door with one hand and, just as he was fleetingly distracted, Poppy succeeded in breaking free and sprang, her jaws snapping ferociously. Even a small dog can cause painful injuries, and her assault was sudden and unexpected. I was dimly aware of a small ball of fur hurling itself at Niles, and then everything was a blur as he fell over, taking me with him. There was a sound of snapping jaws and I felt Niles's grip on my neck tighten for an instant as Poppy sunk her teeth into his forearm, which was pressing against my throat. He let out a piercing scream and loosened his grip. With a panicked cry, I jerked my head free.

After that, it was all over very quickly.

Barry and Adam fell on Niles. They grabbed an arm each, and had him lying face down on the floor, both arms twisted behind his back, before he had a chance to resist. Niles thrashed and kicked out, bellowing with rage, but he was powerless to resist. Barry made no attempt to hide a triumphant smile as he dragged Niles to his feet, and everyone cheered – apart from Niles himself. Barry had no handcuffs with him so he tied Barry's wrists together with a piece of rope Cliff gave him. The fracas woke Maud from her slumber and she sat up quickly, insisting that she wasn't asleep. She gazed in surprise at the chaotic scene.

Hannah and Michelle rushed over to help me scramble to my feet, and check whether Niles had hurt me. I assured them I was fine, but that didn't stop them fussing over me. Hannah supported me to a chair while Michelle brought me a cup of hot sweet tea. When I protested that I never took sugar in my tea, she insisted I drink it all, telling me that it was good for shock. I tried to remonstrate with her, pointing out that Niles was the one who had suffered a shock, not me, but she refused to listen to my protestations and insisted I drink the tea. In the end, it was easier to comply than continue arguing with her, so I drank the whole cup and felt much better for it. Michelle had always struck me as gentle but I saw another side to her that day, and gained an insight into not only her kindness, but also her competence as a carer.

With his red Father Christmas hat askew on his head, and a torn shred of his red cloak still around his neck, Niles glared furiously around the room, snarling imprecations against anyone who approached him. A few of the younger children began pointing at Barry, bleating that he had pushed Santa over, but most of the children were beside themselves with joy, avidly watching the drama playing out in front of them.

'Do it again!' one of them pleaded. 'Do it again!' Another one took up the chant, and soon all the children were clamouring for a repeat performance of my capture and release, and Niles's arrest. 'Make the dog jump up!' they cried out, and 'Catch Santa! Catch Santa!'

'You have to say encora,' one of the older children told them earnestly. 'Clap your hands and shout "encora" and "bravo" and it makes them do more.'

'Encora!' and 'Bravo!' the children all shrieked, applauding and jumping up and down with excitement.

But there was to be no repeat performance of Niles's arrest.

Dana had been watching the drama unfold. Irritated, I realised that before long the whole sorry tale would be splashed all over the local paper. It was probably sensational enough to reach the national news outlets. Surprisingly, I hadn't witnessed Dana taking her phone out, but assumed she had been busy taking photos while I had been preoccupied with the threat to my life.

'I'm sorry', Barry murmured, coming to stand beside me. 'I tried to warn you about Niles, but –'

'But I wouldn't listen,' I finished the sentence for him.

'I should have tried harder,' he said. 'It was difficult.'

It would have been cruel to allow him to blame himself for my stupidity. 'It wasn't your fault,' I insisted quietly.

Before we could continue our conversation, Cliff stepped forward, yanked the hat off Niles's head, and gathered up the ripped cloak which was lying on the floor near the door at the site of my graceless fall.

'Now then, children, now then!' he bellowed, holding the remains of Niles's beard up to his chin. 'Who wants a present from Santa?'

With a dubious glance at Niles, the children formed an untidy queue, urged on by their parents. Michelle found some plasters and managed to attach the remnants of the cotton wool to Cliff's chin. His costume looked ragged and cobbled together, and completely ridiculous, but his smile was broad and cheery. Sensing his jolly mood, the children gathered near him, jostling eagerly, and we heard him telling them about a bit of an upset to his sleigh on his way from Lapland.

'Those silly reindeer overturned my sleigh,' he hollered, so loudly that even the most fretful children stopped crying and drew close to listen. 'My clothes were ripped,' he held up a strip of his red cloak and guffawed, 'but none of your presents was damaged, and that's the main thing. Look!' He reached into the sack and drew out a gift wrapped in red paper. 'So come along, children, line up and get your presents.'

Niles watched sullenly as Cliff handed out presents to each of the children in turn. Hannah was worried there wouldn't be enough but, by some miracle, there were green parcels for all the girls, and red parcels for all the boys. The children seemed content and the parents all thanked Barry and Cliff for saving the party, after which they herded their charges out of the pub, no doubt relieved the party was over. The snow was falling fast now and the children ran into the street, cheering and caterwauling for a snowball fight, their indignation at Father Christmas's ignominy forgotten in the excitement of playing in the snow.

In the calm that followed their departure, we saw the school teacher, Alice, sprawled in a chair, snoring in a drunken stupor. But the Christmas nightmare was not over yet.

Maud stepped forward and glared at Niles, trembling with emotion. 'What have you done with my husband?' she demanded.

23

NILES GRINNED AT MAUD with a careless shrug. 'Well,' he drawled. I felt an involuntary shiver of excitement on hearing his voice, but his next words horrified me. 'If you want your husband back, you'll have to let me go. I mean, you can't really expect to get one without giving up the other. It all depends which you are prepared to sacrifice. Be reasonable,' he went on as Maud started to remonstrate. 'That's only fair, isn't it? An equitable exchange, I'd say,' he concluded with an air of quiet triumph.

Staring at his blue eyes, I shuddered on realising that what I had mistaken for love was instead a cruel passion for pursuing his own selfish desires. Barry leaned forward, putting his face very close to Niles as he formally charged his prisoner with the murder of Chantelle Winters. He warned him that there could be no chance he would be released before he stood trial. If he injured or harmed Norman in any way, Barry went on, there would be clear evidence of premeditation, meaning his sentence would inevitably be harsh. On the other hand, if Niles cooperated in rescuing Norman, he would be able to plead manslaughter due to diminished responsibility for the death of his girlfriend. Barry even guaranteed to personally make sure the judge was lenient when it came to sentencing him.

Niles laughed. 'You can have no power whatsoever over my sentence,' he replied. 'How can you, a piffling police constable, influence a judge? Don't take me for a fool, and don't behave like one either. We both know your only option is to release me, if you want to see Norman alive again.' He turned to Maud. 'Perhaps you can talk some sense into this plod? I suggest you get on with it. Your butcher won't last forever. Of course, none of us will, but his time is running out faster than ours right now.'

'The police are on their way and they'll be here soon,' Barry said.

'They'll have to toboggan here,' Niles laughed.

Maud began to wail, a curious high pitched keening that cut right through me. She rocked backwards and forwards, her arms wrapped around her body as though she was trying to hold on to herself.

'Niles,' Barry said fiercely, 'where is Norman?' I had never seen Barry looking so enraged.

Niles merely leaned back in his seat and grinned. With a shriek, Maud darted forward and hit the side of his head so hard he toppled off his chair, landing on his side with a loud thwack. He squirmed and raised himself into a sitting position on the floor, glaring at her.

'That won't help, you know,' he said in an even tone. 'You know what I want.'

'You can leave him in the cellar here for tonight, if you like,' Cliff said. 'He'll be safe enough in there until your mates can come for him. It'll be freezing cold, mind, and he won't like the rats, but there'll be no risk of him getting away.' He gave an evil grin.

I shuddered, recalling the time I had been trapped in that very same cellar.

Barry nodded. 'It's all right,' he replied. 'We'll keep him where we can see him. And even if he gets away, he can't go far while the streets are impassable.'

'This is inhumane,' Niles protested. 'What happened to innocent until you're proved guilty? Or don't you obey the law? This is going to get you in serious trouble. As for you,' he added, shaking his bound hands at Maud, 'I'll see you sent down for assault.'

'What assault?' Barry retorted. 'I didn't see anyone being assaulted, did you?' He looked around at the rest of us.

Hannah, Adam, Michelle and I all shook our heads. Maud was sobbing too violently to reply.

'I saw you fall off your chair,' Barry went on. 'But I didn't see anyone assaulting you.'

While all this had been going on, Poppy had been looking around, her gaze resting on each of us in turn, almost as though she was counting us. Her puzzled expression gave me an idea.

'Poppy,' I said. 'Where's Norman? You know, the butcher, Norman. Take me to him.'

Poppy put her head on one side, seeming to understand that I wanted her to do something. Then she lay down and rolled onto her back to be petted.

Niles burst out laughing. 'Quite the little bloodhound, isn't she? Or would you say she was more like a vicious rat?'

Spurred on by his insults, I tried again in what was intended to be a voice of command, although it sounded to my ears more like an entreaty. 'Poppy, take me to Norman. You know, Norman, who gives you bones and scraps of meat. Norman, the butcher. We have to find him, Poppy.'

'You're right, Emily,' Barry said, standing up, suddenly brisk. 'We can't just sit around and wait for a search team to arrive. They might not get through for another twenty-four hours. If Norman is exposed to the cold, he's not going to last that long.'

Maud had been looking at us, but now covered her face in her hands and sobbed.

'We should split up and look for him,' Adam suggested. 'I'll try Maud's place. Barry, have you got the key?'

Barry held out a bunch of keys. 'Someone go with him. One of you can search the shop while the other one goes up to the flat.' He showed Adam which key was for each door, and Toby and Adam reached for their coats.

'I'll go to the butcher's in the High Street,' I said and Barry held out another set of keys.

'I'm coming with you,' Hannah announced. 'If he's difficult to shift, you might not manage on your own.'

We discussed whether it might be best for Adam and Toby to accompany Hannah and me, in case we needed help. No one mentioned that even a normal-sized man might struggle to lift Norman's bulk. In the end, we agreed that Michelle and Maud should stay in the pub in case Norman appeared, while Cliff accompanied Hannah and me to the High Street, and Barry went with Adam and Toby. We all checked that our phones were on and had enough battery in case we needed to contact each other.

Before we left, Barry went to tie Niles's ankles together and put a blanket around him, but by the time we had finished discussing what needed to be done, it was too late. While we had been busy arranging to search for Norman, Niles had slipped free of his bonds and vanished. We searched the pub, but there was no sign of him. Barry blamed himself for failing to secure the suspect safely enough when he had the chance, but we all agreed that every one of us was equally culpable. In the few moments when everyone had thought someone else was keeping an eye on Niles, he had vanished without trace, and his footprints were already covered in a layer of snow. Even Poppy would struggle to follow him now. In the meantime, finding Norman had become our immediate priority. If he was tied up outside, he would soon freeze to death. So we set off, our phones ready in case we needed help with Norman, or sighted the killer.

Poppy had been pulling me towards the door since I had told her to find Norman. It was a long shot, but with nothing to lose, I grabbed my coat, hat and gloves, and let Poppy lead me out into the freezing cold, closely followed by the others. Once we were outside, Poppy seemed more interested in the snow than in looking for Norman, if that was what she had intended in the first place. Adam, Toby and Barry set off for Maud's flat, while Hannah and Cliff went on ahead to the butcher's shop. Frustrated by Poppy's refusal to leave the snow outside the pub, where the children had left piles of snowballs and an odd-looking squat snowman, I let her play for a few minutes, digging around and snuffling at the exciting cold terrain. Suddenly, she stood perfectly still, her nose raised in the air. Then she let out a yelp and began running off in the direction of the butcher's.

'Good girl, Poppy,' I cried out. 'Let's go and find Norman.'

I didn't know if she understood me, or whether she was just keen to go home, but I trotted cautiously after her, careful not to slip or lose my balance. Niles could be anywhere, so I was nervous about being out in the street on my own and kept my phone in my hand in case he appeared as I hurried to join Hannah and Cliff. There were lights on inside the butcher's, where Hannah and Cliff were searching for Norman. I tried to restrain Poppy, so that we could join them, but she tugged me on towards the tea shop, ignoring my protests that there was no one there. The fir tree in the centre of the street looked magnificent, and the whole scene was like a real life Christmas card. The strings of fairy lights were shrouded in white, and fresh snow weighed down boughs glittering like tinsel in the moonlight. It was too cold to stay there admiring the beautiful scene, nor did Poppy allow me to linger as she pulled frantically on her lead, seemingly willing to strangle herself before she would give up.

'No, Poppy,' I told her. 'I'm not going to work, you daft thing. We're all looking for Norman. We can't stop now.'

As we drew level with the tea shop, Poppy swerved across the road and tugged me towards the Christmas tree, and the patisserie which had now closed its doors for good.

'There's nothing there, Poppy,' I told her, leaning down to pick her up. 'Let's go back to Norman's and see if Hannah and Cliff have found him yet.'

With a bark of reproof, Poppy wriggled out of my clutches and jumped down onto the snow where she continued pulling me towards the Christmas tree. In the end, I picked her up and carried her back down the street, while she wriggled and fussed to be put down. I kept tight hold of her until we reached the butcher's where I set her down and reached to open the door. As I did so, she gave a sharp tug on the lead which slipped out of my grasp. Before I could stop her, she went haring down the road, back towards the Christmas tree. I hurried off in pursuit, calling her name crossly, but she ran on while I scurried and stumbled after her, nearly falling over more than once. By the time I reached the tea shop, breathless and exasperated, Poppy had disappeared. My frayed temper gave way to unease when I called her but no naughty little dog appeared, frisking in the snow. With increasing alarm I shouted her name repeatedly.

'It's all right, Poppy,' I reassured her anxiously. 'I won't be cross. Come here. Poppy, come! Poppy! Poppy!'

There was silence, apart from a faint scratching sound. Listening carefully, I heard a low whimper which struck me as familiar. Terrified Poppy was hurt, I followed the sound which seemed to be coming from the back of the patisserie. Puzzled and more than a little apprehensive, I shuffled along the side of the building through snow disturbed only by a set of tiny paw prints. The sound of whimpering grew closer. Before long I saw Poppy lying in the snow underneath a window. I hurried over to her and, lifting her in my arms, held her close. The poor creature was wet, and shivering with cold.

'My little Poppy,' I murmured, laying my cheek on her head. 'What's happened to you? Why are you lying here, getting so cold? You can't find shelter leaning against a wall, not in this weather. Come on, let's get you indoors and warm.'

As I began to walk back to the road, Poppy barked and wriggled furiously to be put down. As soon as I let go of her, she leapt out of my arms, darted back and stood up on her hind legs to scratch at the window. Following her along the side of the building, I looked through the window into the darkness of the interior but couldn't see anything. With Poppy so determined to show me what was inside the patisserie, I reluctantly took out my phone. My fingers were so cold, they fumbled to switch on the torch. Peering through the darkness, I had the impression that something moved on the other side of the window. It was difficult to tell in the shadowy interior, but then a vague shape shifted and there was a crash. Something – or someone – was indoors on the other side of the window.

24

SCOOPING POPPY UP IN my arms, I hurried as fast as I could, past the Christmas tree and across the road to the butcher's, only to see my friends Hannah and Cliff leaving. Watching them walking away from me, I shouted to them, but neither of them looked round until Poppy barked loudly at which Hannah finally glanced back and saw us. She spoke to Cliff, after which they both stood still, stamping their feet and slapping their hands together, waiting for me to join them. I yelled at them to follow me, and gesticulated frantically towards the patisserie, but they just stood outside the butcher's waiting for me to catch up with them.

'This way!' I yelled. 'Follow me!'

After what felt like hours, but was really only a couple of minutes, Hannah and Cliff began striding towards me over the snow. Wordlessly I led them along the side wall of the patisserie and shone my phone torch at the window.

'What is it?' Hannah asked. 'What are we doing here? It's too cold to hang around outside.'

'Poppy dragged me here. She insisted we stop by this window and I thought I saw something moving in there.

Then there was a crash. Something's in there and I think it could be Norman. We need to get inside.'

Persuaded by my urgency, Cliff ushered us to the front of the building but the door was locked. We went back to the window and he tried to force it open, but it was no use. While Cliff and I were trying to find a way in, Hannah had been on the phone to Adam. He arrived soon after, along with Barry, who was carrying a crowbar. The rest of us stood back while Barry prised the window open and climbed through it, followed by Cliff. Poppy leapt out of my arms to follow them, and I only just managed to let go of her lead in time, before she could injure herself. Hurriedly I clambered after them. In the light from Barry's torch, I saw Cliff was kneeling down, struggling to untie Norman who lay on the floor beside an overturned chair. His eyes were open and his face looked pale and sweaty.

Switching on the torch on my phone, I hurried past them into the kitchen to search for a pair of scissors. Finding a sharp knife, I ran back with it to help free Norman from his bonds. As we were working, Toby joined us. He phoned Michelle to tell her and Maud that Norman had been found, cold and captive, but unharmed. Carefully, I sliced through the scarf that had been used to gag him, and Norman blurted out his thanks to us for rescuing him. Almost in tears, he described how he had been on his way to the pub, dressed as Father Christmas. As he was passing the patisserie, he saw the front door opening. Niles called out and beckoned to him to enter, explaining he had been sent to intercept Norman on his way to the pub. Niles said he had been asked to hand over the presents Norman was to give to the children. Niles went on to tell Norman that we all thought it would be best for Father Christmas to arrive with the sack on his back; we had blundered in keeping the presents at the pub.

Not realising it was a trap, Norman had cheerfully gone inside to collect the presents. As soon as he crossed the threshold, a bag had been thrown over his head. Before he could react, his costume had been torn off, and his hands and feet had been tied to a chair. He felt as though he had been left there for hours and was beginning to give way to despair, fearing that no one would discover him at least until the morning, by which time he was afraid he would have succumbed to hypothermia.

'I may be fit,' he said, 'but I'm not a young man. And what would have happened to my poor Maud, if I hadn't survived the night?'

When he had heard Poppy whimpering and scratching at the window, he had felt a thrill of hope. Gagged and tied up, he had sat there, trussed up like one of his own Christmas turkeys, powerless to call out or move. As I shone a light through the window, in desperation he had tried to stand up, hoping to somehow shuffle to the window and attract my attention. That was when his chair had fallen over with a crash that, while bruising his shoulder, had quite possibly saved his life by being audible outside.

While he was telling us about his shocking experience, we took it in turns to saw at Norman's restraints, our efforts hampered by the need to avoid injuring him. Finally free, he regarded the welts on his wrists and ankles ruefully. He had rubbed his skin raw against the ropes, vainly attempting to free himself. He also had a nasty bruise on his shoulder from falling off his chair. But he assured us he was otherwise fine, despite having been tied up and left to freeze in darkness for more than an hour in an unheated room.

'I have a natural layer to insulate me against the cold,' he chortled, his good humour restored in his relief at being rescued.

When Barry explained that Niles had been arrested for murdering Chantelle, Norman gasped.

'That's why he trapped you here,' Barry explained, as we started out back to the pub.

It had stopped snowing and the ground was covered in thick freshly fallen snow.

'He knew we were looking for him, and was desperate to evade capture,' Barry went on. 'By disguising himself in your costume, he planned to hide himself in plain sight and escape as soon as the roads out of the village were passable. He might have got away with it, too. Who was going to suspect Father Christmas? Maud had fallen asleep or she would almost certainly have unmasked the imposter. By the time his subterfuge was discovered, he could have been away from the village and impossible to trace.'

'If it hadn't been for Poppy, we wouldn't have found you so soon,' I added.

Norman leaned down to pat her on her head. 'That's a lifetime of juicy bones for you,' he said and she wagged her tail and let out a jubilant bark.

Maud's joy on seeing Norman walk into the pub brought tears to my eyes. She flung herself into his arms, sobbing and laughing hysterically. It was a while before she calmed down enough to let him sit down and tell his tale all over again. With a mug of beer in one huge hand, a hot mince pie in the other, and his complexion restored to its characteristic ruddy colour, he settled down to recount his story to Maud and Michelle, and anyone else who would listen. This time, I noticed a few embellishments to his account. He claimed that he would have easily resisted Niles's attempt to overpower him had the villain not knocked him out with chloroform, and he described huge rats he had seen scurrying around the room where he was held captive. They would, he claimed, have attacked anyone who had not glared at them as fearlessly as he did. Maud hung on his words eagerly, when she wasn't engaged in replenishing his beer and bringing him fresh mince pies.

Barry suggested I put his number on speed dial on my phone in case I saw anything suspicious on my way home. When he offered to accompany me, I accepted at once. Since Niles was still at large, we were all on edge. As we walked along the lane that led to my cottage, Barry told me that snow ploughs and gritting lorries were already out, so the roads from Ashton Mead would be open by the morning. Preparations were under way to start searching for Niles, just as soon as police vehicles could reach the village.

'We still have to catch him,' Barry said, with a rueful smile. 'We're not going to let him get away just because it's snowing.'

He escorted me and Poppy as far as our gate. Grateful for his support, I invited him in for a hot drink but it was late and we were both worn out after the eventful day, so he declined, saying he would see me at the Christmas lunch at the tea shop, unless the manhunt was still going on. Before I had a chance to tell him I hoped he would make it to Hannah's, he turned and strode swiftly away into the dark snowy night, leaving me and Poppy alone at the gate.

I hurried along the path as quickly as I could, treading on snow and carefully avoiding slipping on ice. Poppy hung back and as we reached the front door she began growling, seeming reluctant to go indoors.

'Don't be silly, Poppy,' I told her. 'It's far too cold to stay out here. Come on, we're going in.'

As I opened the door, she pulled on her lead, refusing to go inside. Grumbling, I dragged her into the house and shut the front door behind us. It was a relief to be home and I bolted the door securely. Our walk home in the snow had seemed to take a long time and my legs were aching. Safe and warm at last, I removed my wet shoes and coat, ignoring Poppy's fussing. It took me a moment to register that the light was on in the living room. I was almost certain I had switched it off before I left home earlier. Poppy was still growling softly, making me uneasy. Fumbling for my phone, while reaching for my shoes, I let the lead slip between my fingers. As soon as she was released, Poppy dashed into the living room, barking frantically. I ran after her, and halted in shock.

'Come in,' Niles greeted me with a disarming smile. He put down a mug of tea and rose to his feet in one graceful movement. 'I've been expecting you.'

25

IN THAT INSTANT I remembered that my spare keys were missing and cursed myself for not having realised what had happened earlier. It was too late to remedy my oversight. All I could do now was try to escape, but I couldn't leave without Poppy who was in the far corner of the living room, growling at Niles, evidently trying to shepherd him towards the front door. I called her, but she stayed focused on Niles.

'You'd better give me your phone,' he said, still smiling as though this was a friendly social encounter. 'We don't want you doing anything stupid.'

As he held out his hand, Poppy leapt. Seizing the back of his leg between her teeth, she appeared to be trying to shake him, like one of her toys. He yelled in pain. While he was distracted, I switched on my phone, but before I could press Barry's number, Niles had shaken Poppy off, lunged forward and grabbed it.

'A pointless gesture,' he sneered as he dropped my phone in his mug of tea.

I let out an involuntary groan.

'Now you get lost,' he snapped at Poppy. He went to kick her but she was too quick for him. With an angry cry he picked her up, squirming and snarling, and carried her at arm's length to the front door.

'Open this door!' he yelled at me. 'Open it or I'll wring the little monster's neck.'

This was not the time to point out that *he* was the monster, not Poppy. Trembling, I unbolted the door and pulled it open. Niles hurled Poppy out into the snowy garden and slammed the door shut.

'You can't do that,' I gasped. 'She'll freeze.'

Niles seized me by the arm and propelled me back into the living room where he stood for a moment, rubbing his calf and muttering under his breath. I began edging back towards the front door, with a vague idea of grabbing my shoes and running out to get help. My next door neighbour, Richard, was probably asleep, but if I made enough noise, I might be able to rouse him. Suddenly Niles seemed to recall where he was and turned to me.

'Sit!'

He must have placed one of my long kitchen knives down the side of the sofa earlier, because he drew it out and brandished it in my face. There was a crazed look in his eyes that left me in no doubt that he would stab me if provoked.

'Not there,' he said, as I went to sit on one of my armchairs. He gestured at the sofa.

'I'm going to need a car,' he went on. 'And money.'

'I don't have a car.'

'How much money have you got?' he demanded.

I shook my head. 'Not much,' I admitted.

Helplessly I considered hurling myself at him but, while

he was holding the knife, I didn't dare risk any sudden movement. I sat perfectly still.

'There's no point in taking a car anyway,' I said, surprised at how calm I sounded. 'You won't get anywhere. The roads are closed.'

Niles appeared to be thinking.

'I'll leave at first light,' he said, as though he was sharing his holiday plans. 'The roads should be open by then. In the meantime, we'll be safe here. As long as I can't get out of the village, the police won't be able to get to us. They're as trapped as we are.' He chuckled. 'They're helpless. I just have to get out of the village before they arrive. And they have no idea where I am, which gives me a head start. I'll simply cut across country and slip straight past them and be gone long before you're found.' He nodded briskly at me as though he had reached a decision. 'Go and get me two scarves, no three. No, wait. We'll go upstairs together. I can't have you running out on me, can I?' he added, smiling. 'Or using a phone up there.'

With Niles holding the knife at my throat, we shuffled awkwardly upstairs.

'I've only got one scarf,' I said, 'and that's downstairs.'

'Scarves, stockings, anything. Use your initiative,' he said impatiently. 'Anything I can use to tie you up with. Get a move on. I want to get away as soon as the snow eases up. I'm not leaving in a blizzard.'

As I rummaged through my drawers to find tights and a pashmina, I felt a surge of relief at knowing he wasn't planning to kill me.

A thaw was forecast in a couple of days. In the meantime, the snow ploughs had been busy and soon we would no longer be isolated. Somehow I had to prevent Niles from getting away, but that was going to be difficult once he tied me up. Part of me didn't really care if he escaped. I just didn't want to die. And I wanted Poppy to survive. Still holding the knife at my throat, he propelled me downstairs ahead of him. We descended in a clumsy tandem. At last we were back in the living room, where he lay me down on the floor and sat on me while he tied my ankles together, before he secured my hands and gagged me. Satisfied that I was immobilised and silenced, he ensconced himself on an armchair and sat watching me drag myself onto the sofa.

'As soon as it's daylight, I'm off,' he told me.

We settled down to wait for the morning. Seated on the sofa, gagged and bound, it was impossible to sleep. Time passed very slowly. In the long hours of silence, it was impossible not to worry about Poppy. She was a sturdy little dog, but she would never survive a night outdoors in freezing conditions. I could only hope she had managed to find shelter somewhere. The more I thought about her, shivering and forlorn, the more I hated Niles who had so callously sent her out into the cold to suffer and die. But there was nothing I could do to help her. My legs ached from being held in one position, my shoulders grew stiff, and I needed the toilet, but I couldn't speak and Niles ignored my muffled grunts.

The morning finally dawned. Rising to his feet, Niles went over to the window to peer out.

'Just look how foggy it is,' he crowed, opening the curtain. 'Perfect weather for an escaping fugitive, wouldn't you say?'

He turned round and grinned at me. Had I not been gagged, I would have cried out when he picked up the knife. He appeared to be weighing it in his hand, while he gazed at me thoughtfully. Facing the window, through swirls of mist I made out the shape of a dark van drawing up outside the cottage. And then someone banged loudly at the front door. Niles straightened up as though he had been shot and glared around the room, swearing under his breath. I sat perfectly still, listening. As well as the banging, we heard a loud voice announcing that the house was surrounded. The police had arrived.

But I was more interested in the familiar sound of a dog barking.

'The house is surrounded by armed police officers. You can't get away. Come out with your hands above your head,' the amplified voice called out.

The mist cleared momentarily, revealing a police van parked outside my gate, just as the door burst open with a resounding crash and four uniformed officers rushed in with Poppy at their heels. She ran straight over to me, and began licking my hands. One of the uniformed officers was Barry. Within a few seconds, Niles had been handcuffed while Barry swiftly released me from my bonds. Once he had been reassured that I was unharmed, he explained that Poppy had appeared in the street outside Maud's village store. From his flat above the shop, Barry had been woken by the sound of her frantic barking.

'It wasn't just me. I think she was barking loudly enough to wake the whole street,' he added, grinning at her.

As soon as Barry saw Poppy out in the street on her own, he knew something was seriously amiss. Several vans of police officers had already arrived in the village, preparing to search for Niles. Summoning a group of his colleagues, Barry had driven straight to Rosecroft, arriving in time to stop Niles getting away. My gag had been removed by the time Niles was frogmarched past us, but for once I didn't scold Poppy for barking at him.

'It's all right, Poppy,' Barry said, 'Niles won't be bothering Emily again.' He crouched down to scratch her behind her ears. 'I can't promise to say the same for me though,' he added, just loudly enough for me to hear. As he straightened up, he glanced at me and caught me smiling.

'What's going on now?' I asked him. 'Please say you're not going to Swindon today?'

'Don't worry,' he replied. 'The roads are open again so I can be there and back in no time. I'll see you again soon.'

As he was being dragged to the door, Niles turned.

'Emily,' he called out frantically, 'Emily! Tell them. Ask her,' he told a police officer who was holding him by the arm. 'She'll tell you she was with me at the time the murder took place. She'll tell you. Emily tell them.' His voice rose in desperation. 'Tell them I was with you, Emily, and all this will be over. We can go away together, and – '

Poppy strained forward, growling at him. She barked once, as if in warning, and he glared at her.

'If it wasn't for that brute –' he began.

Barry interrupted him. 'Come on,' he said, 'let's get you to Swindon. Say goodbye to Niles,' he added, looking down at Poppy. 'This is the last you're going to see of him.'

Poppy wagged her tail and turned away to nuzzle my feet. She had lost interest in Niles already. It would take me longer to get over him but, unlike Poppy, I had never really known him. I had been infatuated with a false idea of Niles created out of my own longing for romance.

26

FOR A COUPLE OF weeks I was inconsolable, and unable to sleep. Gradually, with the support of my close friends, I began to come to terms with my shock at the exposure of Niles's evil duplicity. Without the comforting presence of my little dog, it would have taken me far longer to recover from my distress. Hannah was sympathetic, but she refused to accede to my demand to take time off work, insisting that she was too busy to manage without me. Her decision turned out to be the right one for me, which had no doubt been her intention, as working helped to keep my mind off my disappointment. Admitting responsibility for my own part in the disaster was probably the hardest thing to bear. Forced to confront my own naïveté, I couldn't help but feel devastated by what had happened. I had fallen for men's lies before, but had never realised quite how poor a judge of character I was.

I discussed my shortcomings with Hannah one day in the tea shop as we were sitting over a pot of tea before clearing up at the end of the day.

'What happened is absolutely no reflection on you,' she said firmly. 'That guy was a professional conman. He took everyone in. It's perfectly understandable that you fell for his charms. Anyone would have done the same, in your position.'

Poppy barked.

'Okay, everyone fell for his lies apart from Poppy,' she conceded, smiling at her and slipping her a crumb of scone. 'You weren't taken in for a moment, were you?' She leaned down to pet Poppy before straightening up and addressing me again. 'Listen to me, everyone, apart from your dog, was completely fooled by him. Everyone. What I want to know is, how did Poppy know not to trust Niles?' she went on, as I sipped my tea. 'It's quite unbelievable, when you think about it.'

I shook my head. 'She's just possessive over me, that's all.'

Hannah reiterated that she was mystified by Poppy's uncanny powers.

Looking down at Poppy, I wasn't sure it was really so difficult to understand her ability. 'You do know she's very clever,' I said. 'Just because she can't talk, and her intelligence isn't like ours, doesn't mean she can't be smarter than us when it comes to judging people.'

Hannah grunted dismissively. 'You're talking about a dog,' she replied. 'But whatever you say,' she added quickly, seeing that I was about to protest, and we left it at that.

Out of respect for the dead, Hannah held back from gloating aloud, but she was clearly delighted that the patisserie had closed for good. The estate agent wasted no time in removing the neon lights and brightly coloured signs and displaying a 'To Let' notice on the front of the premises. Once again, speculation was rife about who would take over. There was only a very remote chance that another café would open up in the High Street, and we were cautiously confident that we would face no repetition of the competition that had recently dented Hannah's profits. For no reason that I could ascertain, most people in the village seemed to think it was going to be a shoe shop or a barber's. Time would tell. In the meantime, nothing was going to happen before Christmas so there was no point in worrying about it, and we were free to concentrate on our preparations for the festivities.

As time elapsed between the Children's party and Christmas, we were busy at the tea shop, but I was under pressure with my own preparations. With everything that had been going on, I hadn't yet got around to buying presents for my friends and family. Making a list, I was slightly shocked to see how much I still had to do. One afternoon, Hannah reluctantly gave me time off to go into Swindon to do some Christmas shopping.

'You know I can't really manage without you,' she said.

Jane agreed to cover for me, and Hannah said she wouldn't dock my pay, seeing as it was Christmas and the season of goodwill. She could afford it, now the tea shop was busy again. Leaving Poppy with Holly, I took the bus into Swindon. Perhaps I shouldn't have been surprised to see so many people swarming around the shopping centre just five days before Christmas. Even though it was early afternoon on a Monday, there were queues everywhere. I toyed with the idea of turning round and going straight back home to do my shopping online. The trouble was, having left it so late, there was no firm guarantee that all my purchases would arrive in time for Christmas Day. The prospect of failing to hand gifts to my family and friends was too mortifying to contemplate. Metaphorically girding my loins, I entered the fray, concentrating on the bargain stores which were, of course, the busiest of all.

Other than my father and brother-in-law, my family were quite straightforward. Even if I had a clue about what sort of gift might be appreciated by a teenager, my nephew had reached an age where money was the most practical present. He was easy, as were my mother and sister. Women were always easier to buy presents for. Constrained by how much I could carry, as well as by my limited budget, I chose some attractive woolly hats and matching gloves for my mother and sister, and scarves for my father and brother-in-law. The gifts weren't exactly imaginative, but there was no time to scour the shops for anything personal. I followed the same idea for my friends, partly because it reduced the number of queues I had to join at various tills. Only Hannah was really problematic, because I really wanted to give her something special. Without spending a lot of money, it was difficult to know what to get for her. In the end, I settled for a mirror in a frame decorated with brightly painted carved daffodils. It wasn't very big, as I needed to carry it home along with all my other purchases, but I thought she could hang it on the wall in the Sunshine Tea Shoppe. I hoped she would like it.

In some ways, it was a stressful afternoon, choosing gifts and waiting in a succession of lines to pay for them. My items were modest but even so it was astounding how the cost mounted up. At last I finished, and lumbered along to the bus stop with bags that were not too heavy but bulky and extremely awkward to carry. Had I thought about it more carefully, I would have brought along a case on wheels to transport all my purchases. As it was, I managed with difficulty to manoeuvre my way along the aisle to a seat on the bus and at last I reached home, exhausted but relieved to have completed my challenging mission. Having dumped all my bags, I went to collect Poppy.

'I popped back to take them out a couple of times,' Jane told me, 'and Poppy's been as good as gold.'

Finally we were home and I flopped down on the sofa with a cup of tea and a scone which Hannah had given me from that day's baking.

'Shopping is exhausting,' I told Poppy, and she wagged her tail, her eyes glued to the scone on my plate. 'I'm definitely not going to leave it so late to do my Christmas shopping next year.'

Poppy put her head on one side and gazed at me quizzically, as though she remembered hearing me say exactly the same thing the previous year.

27

By Christmas Eve the snow had all gone although it was still icy out overnight. Hannah and I closed early and were just clearing everything away when my parents arrived, bundled up in thick winter coats, woolly hats, gloves and fur-lined boots. A blast of freezing air blew in as they came through the door and Hannah hurried over to close it behind them before we lost too much heat. Having removed their outermost layers, my parents joined us for a sandwich and a cup of tea to warm them up before we all set off for the pub. They were relieved to have arrived safely, as the weather was looking ominous again. My mother was well turned out, as usual. When I admired my father's Christmas jumper, he explained sheepishly that my mother had insisted he wear it. The jumper clearly hadn't been chosen by my quiet, modest father who usually wore drab grey or navy. He put a brave face on it, but looked faintly uncomfortable in a startlingly bright green jumper sporting a vermilion reindeer with a goofy grin.

My mother gazed around with obvious approval at the tinsel and baubles we had put up, and declared that the tea shop looked positively magical. Fortified by rolls baked that morning, generously filled with ham, cheese, chicken, and egg mayonnaise, and plenty of freshly brewed tea, we put on our coats, hats and gloves again and set off on the short walk up the High Street to the pub, leaving my parents' luggage at the tea shop to be collected on our way home later.

'Watch out for ice,' Hannah warned us.

My mother took my arm and walked with me. 'So when are we going to meet this new boyfriend of yours?' she asked.

I sighed, but there was no point in delaying telling her my news. 'You won't,' I replied shortly and changed the subject. I told her about the party Cliff had hosted for the village children, and about Norman, the butcher, who had agreed to play the role of Father Christmas but been unaccountably held up on his way, leaving the landlord to take over. We had all chipped in to pay for small presents for the children and the children had all enjoyed themselves.

'You really do feel at home here, don't you?' she remarked, a trifle wistfully.

'I love it here,' I answered honestly.

With a sigh, she admitted that she could understand why I liked living in Ashton Mead.

'It's such a peaceful place,' she said wistfully. 'Your father and I thought you would find it dull, seeing as nothing ever happens here. We thought you'd soon get fed up with village life, but I can see it has a certain attraction. It certainly looks beautiful in the winter.'

We didn't stay late at the pub as more snow had been forecast, and as I walked back down the High Street with my parents, past the colourful lights on the shops and the beautifully illuminated Christmas tree, it was hard to believe that anything distressing ever happened in this picturesque village I had grown to love.

My sister arrived very late on Christmas morning, with my brother-in-law and my nephew, Joel, in tow. Blonde, with casually tousled hair, Susie accepted a glass of mulled wine gratefully, before launching into a breathless apology about the terrible weather they had encountered on their way to Ashton Mead. Poor visibility had delayed their arrival by at least a couple of hours, and at one point they had feared they would miss our Christmas celebrations altogether. I told her how we had literally been cut off recently, caught unprepared by an unexpectedly severe blizzard which had thankfully not lasted long. Having exchanged catastrophic weather stories, we agreed how pleased we were to be together, in spite of the bad weather.

'I'm really glad you could make it,' I said.

'We wouldn't have missed this for the world,' she replied, waving her arms around at the festively decorated tea shop. 'It looks fabulous. And it's so lovely to all be together on Christmas Day.' She smiled at my mother before giving me a warm hug.

Knowing how hard my mother had worked to persuade Susie to spend Christmas in Ashton Mead, I smiled. Even without the mulled wine, which had clearly retained enough alcohol to enhance everyone's enjoyment of the day, we would have been a merry company.

'Either I've shrunk, or you've grown taller,' I told my nephew.

'You say that every time you see me,' he laughed.

'That's because you keep growing.'

'You do know people shrink when they get old?' he teased me, and I frowned in mock outrage.

He laughed again, before turning his attention to Poppy. He petted her and she gazed up at him adoringly, trotting devotedly at his heels wherever he went. I didn't blame her for wanting to follow him around. He liked pretending to growl at her and grab her toys, but he was gentle, and she obviously enjoyed his games. I didn't know Alice very well, but had always thought she seemed very nice, and I was pleased when she turned up. We chatted about my employment at the tea shop, and why Alice had gone into teaching.

'Here's hoping next year is a better year for us all,' she said to me, with a smile.

I wondered about her circumstances, and why she had been planning to spend Christmas Day on her own before Hannah had invited her to join us. To my dismay, Dana Flack walked in. Muttering my excuses to Alice, I went to look for Hannah. I found her in the kitchen busily basting a gigantic turkey.

'Dana?' she repeated, without turning round. 'What about her?'

'Why has she come here?'

'She's moved from Swindon and is living somewhere near here,' Hannah answered vaguely.

'But what's she doing *here*, with us?' I repeated.

'I think she's trying to make friends. She told me she was going to be on her own today, so of course I invited her to join us. It didn't seem right to leave her all alone, today of all days.'

I had heard enough, and interrupted her. 'You realise she's only here to spy on us?'

'Spy on us? What on earth are you talking about? Are you pissed already?'

'You do know that everything we say and do will be noted down and reported in her bloody paper?' I demanded, furious that I was going to be forced to spend the entire day on tenterhooks, hoping my mother wouldn't say something tactless about the village.

'She just wants to gather more dirt on the murder.'

'Oh no, you're wrong about that.' Hannah shook her head. 'Poor Dana. She lived for that paper. I don't think she has any idea what she's going to do now.'

Momentarily baffled, I asked her what she meant.

'Poor Dana,' Hannah repeated. 'She's lost her job. She told me the editor of her crummy newspaper let her go. I think that's what she called it.' She sighed. 'Poor Dana.'

Surprised by what she had told me, I gazed at her for a moment, but this was no time to dwell on Dana's situation, while Hannah was preoccupied with the food. I returned to the party, where Maud had launched into an account of her honeymoon, starting with a detailed description of the flight. She had reached her description of the complimentary orange juice on the plane, when Norman took over, giving us a rather livelier account of the holiday. Apparently he had sighted a shark in the ocean and had to shout at a group of swimmers to return to the shore. We were all content to listen to his colourful account of the incident while we were waiting for the turkey to arrive. Probably nothing about Norman's tale would have stood up to scrutiny, but he obviously enjoyed relating his anecdotes, and while his account might have lacked veracity, it was told with infectious enthusiasm.

My mother came over to talk to me. 'You still haven't told me what happened to the new boyfriend we were going to meet.'

I glanced around. Everyone else was busy chatting.

'There is no boyfriend,' I replied, speaking so softly that only she could hear me. 'Not anymore. There was, but it didn't work out.'

'Oh dear, not again.' She sighed and patted my arm. 'I'm so sorry.'

'Don't be,' I told her. 'There's no need to feel sorry for me. Believe me, I'm better off without him.'

'You say that every time,' she said sceptically. 'But –'

'There are no buts about it, and no regrets. Not with this one.'

It was time to take our places at the table. Maud latched on to my mother. Clearly delighted to have a new audience, she started giving my mother details of her recent wedding and my mother seemed to enjoy hearing all about it. When we were all seated, Joel suggested pulling crackers and everyone joined in. Poppy didn't even flinch as we laughed and shouted, and the crackers banged. There followed the usual reading of poor jokes and silly puns and the donning of paper hats. Maud asked me to swap my hat with hers, as I had a bright pink one that matched the dress she was wearing. In the midst of all the merriment, there was a sudden hush around the table as Adam brought in the turkey. Poppy barked joyfully, as though to remind us all that she was there. I shared her excitement. A turkey like that was enough to make anyone feel hungry. It was monumental, golden brown and steaming, and the aroma made my mouth water. Poppy began jumping up and down, unable to contain her impatience.

'I think she wants me to put the turkey on the floor where she can get at it,' Adam laughed.

'Don't worry,' Hannah said, looking down at Poppy with an affectionate smile. 'There's plenty for everyone, including you. You just have to sit and wait.'

Reassured that she wouldn't be overlooked, Poppy obediently sat down, and I could have sworn she was smiling. Our plates were soon piled high with turkey, brussels sprouts, crispy potatoes, pigs in blankets, bread sauce, stuffing, cranberry sauce, and all the trimmings of a traditional Christmas dinner.

'Happy Christmas, Poppy,' I murmured, reaching down to pet her as she waited for her food.

Her tail wagged, but her eyes didn't move from my plate until Hannah placed a bowl heaped with turkey on the floor in front of her.

'Here you are, Poppy. This is for you,' Hannah said. 'It's Christmas. You can eat as much as you like.'

When we had all finished eating, the conversation drifted back to the recent murder. Almost everyone expressed their shock and surprise that Niles had turned out to be a killer. Only Norman claimed to have known there was something dodgy about him right from the start.

'As a butcher,' he said, leaning back in his chair and gazing expansively at the company around the table, 'as a butcher I deal with customers from all walks of life, and I've learned to see straight through people. There's nothing that gets past me.' He grinned and tapped the side of his large nose with one stubby finger.

'He's embarrassed about having been duped and overpowered by Niles,' Hannah whispered to me when I was in the kitchen helping her to fetch a large Christmas pudding, which she was serving with a choice of brandy butter, cream and ice cream. 'He's trying to save face by pretending he saw through Niles, when of course he didn't. None of us did.'

We agreed it was unnecessary for Norman to try and cover up for his own gullibility. Everyone had been taken in by Niles, me especially. For all his charm, he had been nothing more than a slick conman.

We returned to the party and Hannah began serving. 'There are jugs of cream and bowls of brandy butter on the table,' she said.

The others were still talking about the recent murder.

'He nearly got away with it,' Maud said, looking sombre. 'If it hadn't been for Poppy...'

'Yes, trust Poppy to crack the case,' Barry agreed.

'Poppy's a Christmas cracker,' Adam quipped, and for once everyone laughed at his silly joke.

As for Poppy, she was gazing at a plate of pigs in blankets on the table. No one raised an eyebrow as I took one and broke it into small pieces for her to eat.

At last we had all finished the obligatory Christmas Day overeating. Poppy was ready to go outside, so Barry took her with him when he walked to the pub with everyone else, leaving Hannah and me to do some initial clearing up without interruption. After stacking the dirty crockery in the kitchen and storing the leftover food in the fridge or the larder, which took a while, Hannah and I set off to join our friends. At the pub, I walked over to fetch Poppy and so found myself standing at the bar next to Barry. He glanced up at a sprig of mistletoe, and then looked at me questioningly. As I smiled and moved closer to him, I saw Poppy wag her tail.

Acknowledgements

I would like to thank everyone on the team at The Crime and Mystery Club for their continuing support for The Poppy Mystery Tales: Ion, Claire, Ellie, Lisa and Sarah. A special thanks to Demi for all her support. My thanks also go to Steven for his meticulous proofreading, and to Steve for his lovely cover design incorporating Phillipa's brilliant original artwork. Producing a book is a team effort, and I am very fortunate to have such a dedicated team to help me. I have a sneaking suspicion they do all the hard work, while I just play with Poppy and indulge my passion for storytelling.

I would like to add my special thanks to the readers who have contacted me to say how much they are enjoying meeting Poppy in her Mystery Tales.

As for the real 'Poppy', I wish you health and happiness in a life filled with treats and long walks in the grass.

If you enjoyed *Poppy's Christmas Cracker*, don't miss the other Poppy Mystery Tales!

After losing her job and her boyfriend, Emily is devastated. As she is puzzling over what to do with the rest of her life, she is surprised to learn that her great aunt has died, leaving Emily her cottage in the picturesque Wiltshire village of Ashton Mead. But there is one condition to her inheritance: she finds herself the unwilling owner of a pet. Not knowing what to expect, Emily sets off for the village, hoping to make a new life for herself.

When Emily decides to investigate the mysterious disappearance of a neighbour, she unwittingly puts her own life in danger...

When Emily stumbles on the body of a woman who apparently drowned in the river, the other villagers suspect foul play and are quick to blame Richard, Emily's next-door neighbour and a newcomer to the village. Emily finds it hard to believe her friendly neighbour could be a cold-hearted murderer, and when she meets Richard's attractive son, Adam, her feelings only become more complicated.

Determined to find out the truth behind the death in the village, Emily travels to London to track down the man with whom Richard's wife was having an affair.

Unlike the other residents of Ashton Mead, Silas Strang and his mother have a bad reputation. Rude and aggressive, they terrorise their neighbours and no one stops them. That is until Silas sets his sights on Emily's beloved dog Poppy, which Emily won't stand for. After a public altercation, Silas is mysteriously murdered. To Emily's dismay, the police view her as their number one suspect.

Assisted by her friends, Hannah and Toby, Emily sets out to establish the truth and clear her name... but her enquiries have frightening consequences.

'Fun and heartwarming with all the mystery and tight plotting you'd expect from Leigh Russell'
VICTORIA SELMAN, *Sunday Times* bestselling author of *Truly, Darkly, Deeply*

'Fast-paced, fun and featuring a fiendish puzzle'
CRIME FICTION LOVER

'All dog lovers will love this fun read cosy crime... full of mystery [and] romance. I look forward, very much, to Poppy and Emily's next outing'
MYSTERY PEOPLE

CRIMEANDMYSTERYCLUB.CO.UK/LEIGH-RUSSELL

Sign up to The Crime & Mystery Club's newsletter
to get a FREE eBook:

crimeandmysteryclub.co.uk/newsletter